RES

For those who worry about the future...

CHAPTER ONE

Randdol Mupt hated Tuesdays. He also hated all the other days of the week, but it just so happened today was Tuesday, so for today, Tuesday was the day he hated most.

He hated that on the walk home at night, the streets were bright, tinted with blue diffused lights that left no shadows. When he was a boy, an ambiance permeated the night. Deep shadows in the recesses between the lights, dark alleyways, and sketchy underpasses.

It was a boon that crime was down. Muggers, rapists, and vagrant scum didn't exist in Hata. The price for the safety was that no matter the time of day The Brigade watched and for that they needed constant light.

If he still had it, Randdol would give his left testicle for one night of darkness, one night where the life of the city calmed and there was peace—no lights or sounds. It was bad enough having the constant wordcast played in his ears, a literal soundtrack to his life.

It was pre-evening affirmation, so the music that streamed into his head contained the typical upbeat rhythm. The bouncy sound of a piano played with a melody that skipped forward, most likely to remind those on their way home from work that their day was over, or to attempt perking-up those who were working late for the extra credit hours.

Stepping off the sidewalk, the rubber heel of Randdol's cane caught along the lip of a pothole. His faux leather oxford shoes tottered on the concrete, and he shifted his weight to not lose balance. For a man of his age, he was still nimble. He only used the cane because he'd misplaced the big toe on his right foot. He lost it and half his pointer toe in the last war, and the cane was for balance, not strength. It cost him a smidge of pride to use it, but he refused to be one of those senior types that broke a hip falling off a couch or curb.

Half a block ahead, a glass door to a connivance store slammed open with enough force to shatter the glass against the brick exterior of the building. A big man, younger than Randdol, maybe in his fifties, burst through the door, being chased by a younger woman swinging a broom. The shaft of the broom busted over the older man's head and the woman kicked him, sending him rolling down the stairs.

"You're a cacking cuck!" The man crawled away, in a clear attempt to escape the rampaging woman's blows.

"I want my credit hours." The woman, dressed in a see-through blue nighty, stomped in front of the groveling man, thwarting his retreat. A light gust of wind ruffled her silk slip. Giving Randdol a flash of naked flesh.

"Watch it," the man said. "You make a ruckus and you know what'll happen. I ain't getting sent away for you."

Randdol turned his back to the whole affair. Although passing the connivance store was the fastest route to his apartment, getting tangled in a situation like the one unfolding was dangerous.

Of course, there was no darkness in the streets. The Brigade would already be on their way. What would happen if he fled without reporting it? That could make him just as guilty.

Randdol pinched the webbing between his left thumb and

pointer finger. He felt the hard, coin-like disk under his skin, and as he pushed down, it quivered with brief haptic feedback.

The music of the wordcast dimmed in his ears.

"What can I do for you, citizen?" a voice asked directly into his head.

"There's a crime in progress," Randdol said.

"Hold please, while I triangulate your position."

The wordcast music was almost inaudible. If it wasn't so risky calling in The Brigade, Randdol would do it more often just to have a moment of quiet.

"Thank you, citizen," the voice said. "Brigaders have already been dispatched to your location and should arrive... now."

The private cast ended, and the music returned to full volume. Before Randdol could manage a sigh, a thumping sound rang from above.

A single hoverlift zoomed over the tops of the skyscrapers. Its pod-shaped body resembled an insect with glowing knobs, adding red lights to the bright night. The hoverlift dodged an overpass and parked in the center of the street.

"Look what you've done now!" the man on the ground half-yelled and half-laughed at the almost naked woman. "You are going to get it."

Four brigaders exited the lift, each with their guns drawn. The hoverlift lights danced across the polished white weapons as three surrounded the man and the woman in perfect step while the fourth bee-lined toward Randdol.

The brigaders' armor was gunmetal black with kevlar pads along the chest and joints. Under the bulk of it hid the person's form, so that theoretically any brigader could be a man or woman, though Randdol had never heard of a female brigader.

The brigaders carried a gun and several grenades, but the real threat was their helmets. The equipment wrapped around their entire heads, hiding all their facial features. A respirator covered their neck and mouth to protect against chemical warfare. It also distorted their voices, making them all sound alike. The dome of helmet was a reflective black, and speckled across it, like barnacles, were nubby white lights that made the brigaders resemble bugs.

Supposedly, the helmets gave the brigaders a full 360-view and provided other augmented information, like revealing full background checks, heart rates, blood pressure, and other idiosyncrasies that gave them sage-like powers.

"Randdol Mupt." The brigader didn't so much ask his name as state it, letting Randdol know they were aware of who he was. "Our records show you took almost a minute and twenty seconds to report the street crime you witnessed."

"Sorry, sir." Randdol hunched his back, leaning on his cane, doing his best to emphasis his use of it. "At my age, my eyes and wits are not what they appear to be. It took me a moment to process what I had seen."

"Complacency is not allowed."

"I know, sir."

In front of the connivance store, the three brigaders had handcuffed the woman and were escorting her to the hoverlift. Randdol shook his head, disgusted. Physical assault was one of the worst crimes one could commit. There was no doubt about what would happen to the woman. They'd transport her to one of the labor cities to work until she died.

They released the man, who'd refused to pay the woman for her services, and he took no time to hustle down the empty street, putting as much distance as possible between himself and The Brigade members. Theft of service carried a minimal fine in Hata. He might work a few extra credit hours, but as long as he stayed clean, nothing would catch up to him.

"We won't warn you again," the brigader said to Randdol. "Next time you see an assault, you call it in immediately."

"Yes, sir," Randdol said. The whole situation was a shame. The woman should have never hit the man, at least not where someone was watching, and in Hata, someone was always watching.

CHAPTER TWO

Assistant Warden Catherine Tayes hopped onto the hoverlift. From the cabin door she watched as Randdol Mupt hobbled down the street. His recent records were clean, but he was trouble. She had one task in Hata: to keep the peace. Failure in that meant sanctions, or worse, and she knew Mupt threatened that.

In the hoverlift's brig, the connivance store employee thrashed about, pounding her fist on the unbreakable tempered glass window. Tayes chuckled, repeating "connivance store employee" in her head. She still thought of the woman as a prostitute, even if no one else acknowledged it. No matter how much clothing, ribbons, jewels, or perfume were used to gussy up a pig, the truth remained: a pig is still a pig.

The incident at the connivance store was the third assault arrest this week. A joke around The White Tower was those who philosophically opposed Hata were lacing the city's water with drugs. The rumors gained so much traction that Warden Hobbes had ordered brigaders to stand watch over the Hata's water filtration system, which created a self-fulfilling prophecy. Fewer brigaders on the street meant a rise in assaults.

The hum of the hoverlift's engines softened as the shuttle hit maximum height and glided across the city. With the building and people below looking like toys, Hata appeared deceptively peaceful. Built on the triangular tip of a peninsula, the city was surrounded on two sides by a bay. On the third side, where the peninsula met land, stood a mighty white wall built decades ago to keep out The Opposition.

"We've been cleared for landing pad 19-X," the pilot said to Tayes.

"Take her in." Tayes shifted to see out the front of the hoverlift. Dead ahead stood The White Tower, the tallest building in the world and the only structure in Hata higher than the wall. Tayes had always thought The White Tower looked like an upside-down champagne flute, with a bulkier base that slimmed to a stem and then bulged out with a halo at its top. The building glowed, its outer walls made from luminescent panels filled with pure white light—a stunning contrast to the constant blue lights of the surrounding city.

A moment before the hoverlift touched the landing pad, Tayes' boots hit it. She drew her gun and waited. Her helmet's heads-up display already showed an increased heart rate for the arrested woman. That wasn't surprising. Being dragged to The White Tower was intimidating and scary. But what had caught Tayes' attention was the spiking graph representing the woman's blood pressure. That was abnormal.

The three junior brigaders dragged the prisoner down the hoverlift's ramp. Like a feral cat refusing a bath, the woman kicked and screamed, trying to break free. In the chaos of her movement, the woman swiped a gun off one the brigader's belts.

Tayes was ready for it. The others should have been.

Pulling her trigger finger, Tayes let loose a single spike from her gun. The stake-like projectile drove into the prisoner's chest, just below her clavicle. Arcs of lightning scattered from the stake, spreading across the woman's body. The woman struck the landing pad and flopped around as if having a seizure.

It looked violent, but Tayes had dialed her gun to the minimum setting. The woman would wake up with a minor wound on her chest and feeling dehydrated, but otherwise she'd be unharmed.

"Lock her up in Quarter B." Tayes holstered her gun. "And next time watch your HUDs for signs of something like this."

Leaving the subordinates to deal with the clean-up, Tayes crossed the landing pad and waved her left hand in front of the airlock's control panel. The webbing between her pointer and thumb vibrated, acknowledging that her tag had been read and processed.

The lower levels of The White Tower were hermetically sealed and set at a minus two PSI, meaning there was almost no wait from when the airlock door shut behind Tayes and the one in front of her opened. Now and then she would feel lightheadedness, but most often that only occurred when she was dealing with a sinus infection or bad allergies.

Tayes used her HUD to summon a lift to take her to the fifty-second floor. Most of the levels below that housed tech services, offices, the cafeteria, and living quarters for brigaders.

The lift hurled upward, and with the standardized pressure of the building, her ears didn't pop. The doors to the lift opened to a plain lobby with all white furniture. It was a theme that spread through the mega-skyscraper. Someone somewhere must have thought it would be funny to have everything inside The White Tower also be white.

Stopping by her office, Tayes snapped off her helmet. The back hood flipped up and the sides bloomed out, releasing her short sable-colored hair that was only a shade lighter than her skin. She set the helmet down on a stack of papers covering her desk. About half of which she hadn't even bothered to sort through yet.

She tucked her short bob behind her ears, much preferring to wear her helmet, since it kept her hair out of her eyes, but she had to meet with Hobbes, and Hobbes always acted more suspicious when she had the helmet on, as if he worried about what she might be deducing with it.

"Oh, Catherine, I thought that was you," Barbra Peters said.

Barbra, who always wore a genuine smile, leaned on the glass doorframe of the office. Her hair was curled in an old style like Tayes' mother used to wear.

"It's me." As annoying as Barbra was, she was harmless and a hard worker. She was also the closest thing that Tayes had to a peer. Where Tayes ran The Brigade outside The White Tower, Barbra handled them on the inside, always worrying about food supplies, schedules, credit hours, and all the junk that Tayes didn't want to touch.

"How are things with the citizens?" Barbra added an extra syllable, dragging out the word citizens, as if trying to make it sound fancier then it was. "Are they behaving?"

"Same old same old," Tayes said. "How are the grandkids?"

"Let me show you!" Barbra clapped and waved for Tayes to follow. "You will not believe how big Anna is getting!"

"Oh, I would love to look at holovids," Tayes said. "But I really should be getting in to see Hobbes. I'm sure he's expecting me."

Barbra looked down the hallway. Her eyes narrowed, and then she nodded as if agreeing. "He is in a bit of a mood today."

"I'll stop by after meeting with him. Okay?"

Barbra grinned. "That would be great."

Tayes did her best to swallow her impatience and walked down the lonely hallway to Hobbes' office. Paintings and awards lined the walls. A few holovids even autoplayed as Tayes passed them.

Bright light stabbed Tayes' eyes as she pushed open the door to Hobbes' office. She blinked, and as her pupils adjusted, she saw Hobbes sitting at his desk. Behind him, the floor-to-ceiling windows were ablaze with light from the luminescent panels on the exterior of the building.

"Sir." Tayes sat down at a chair across from his desk, her armor squeaking against the stained cherry wood.

Hobbes raised his left hand, shutting down his computer monitors. They dimmed, allowing him to see through them. "Three assaults in one week is bad."

"We're doing our best," Tayes said. "I have tech crews around the clock monitoring the citizens."

"I don't care about the assaults. Things happen, what I do care about are the stats. One more incident and there is no way I can prevent the upstairs from hearing about them."

"That would be bad."

"I give you freedom. That's how this works. You handle the city, Barbra handles management things here, and I handle the upstairs. But this is a deal breaker. You understand what I'm saying?"

"Yes." Tayes didn't agree, but arguing with Hobbes would do her no good. "But I think you should consider shutting down the connivance stores."

"That's not going to happen."

"Half of the incidents in the city can be—"

"You and I don't make those kinds of rules. The Word created them and as much as I'm not a fan of them, they provide control."

"They promote violence. It's not—"

"The secret to keeping people happy in Hata is simple. Sex and food. Put nourishment in their bellies, give them an orgasm, and you can get them to do anything. Those two simple things are all you need to keep control."

"It's not working. The—"

"Then make it work." Hobbes stood, turning sideways, his thin frame silhouetted by the white light. "If assault numbers keep rising, this whole city is in trouble."

Tayes nodded, not trusting herself to use words. If she did, they'd be the kind that could possible lead to her being detained, and what good would being locked in a cell do? Letting loose on Hobbes, just once, would feel so good, but not today. Today she would keep quiet.

CHAPTER THREE

As soon as Randdol was close enough for the sensor to pick up his tag, the doors to his apartment complex slid open. That was a good thing for a crappy Tuesday. It wasn't unusual for the power grid to quiver. When that happened, he had to force the sliding doors open with a crowbar he kept hidden under a storm runoff grate.

Randdol lived on the ninth floor, and although he hated the chore of climbing the stairs twice a day, they kept him fit whereas other men his age grew rounder and weaker in their indolence. There was also a sense of pride that came with living so high. Sure, there were plenty of taller apartments, but at his he was on the penultimate floor and that brought respect.

In his head, the wordcast played a pop violin number. The music drowned out his footsteps as he climbed the deserted stairwell, though now and then he could make out the ringing sound his metal cane made when it twanged across the concrete.

Registering him, the door to his apartment opened and the kitchen light kicked on. The studio was laid out in an L-shape. The kitchen flowed into the living area, which was also where he slept, and to the right side was his bathroom.

Randdol's stomach rumbled. Thanks to the incident outside the connivance store, he was running late. Most nights he would have eaten dinner and already been settling down for the evening affirmation.

He hooked his cane onto a rack by the door and used the quartz kitchen counter to support himself. Swinging a cabinet open, he stared at stacks of food cartridges. Mashed peas stew crammed the whole bottom shelf, while shepherd marsala filled the second, and on the top shelf sat a single cartridge of flame-grilled steak patty.

Steak patty had been common enough back in the day, but now it was a rarity. This cartridge had been a reward last year for doubling his estimated quota at work. He'd been saving it for a special occasion, and considering he came face to face with The Brigade and walked away, he felt rather special.

His finger stroked the steak patty cartridge, but he didn't pick it up. Although he should be jubilated for escaping the brigaders, today wasn't any different from yesterday. He'd save the steak patty for a real celebration, for a day where he'd earned it. Giving the cartridge one last look, he let it plop back on the shelf and settled for some mashed peas stew.

Randdol waved his tag-hand over his MicroPot. The dome-shaped device sparked to life and its top retracted. He set the cartridge in and waved his hand over it a second time. The MicroPot closed, hissed for ten seconds, and reopened, reveling his rejuvenated stew.

It smelled like cack, but food was food. The pasty brown substance had an aftertaste like shoe rubber, and he ate it for the sake of nourishment rather than enjoyment. In the past, he spent the energy to pretend the stew tasted like a steak patty. He told himself it wasn't worth the effort, but to be honest, it had been so long he couldn't quite remember the taste of steak patty, just that it was his favorite.

He threw the empty cartridge into the recycler just as the music playing in the wordcast faded away. That meant it was 8:01 and time for the evening affirmation. Through the cast, he heard the voice of The Word. Out of habit, Randdol mouthed the words along with the voice.

"Resist them. Trust The Word. The Word will not lie. It is loyal to you. It wants you great. It wants you safe from The Opposition. The Opposition wants to take. They want your freedom. They want your thoughts. They want you. The Opposition will come. When it does, resist them."

Trumpets rang out as other brass instruments crescendoed into a fanfare before melting into the quiet of soft piano, an audible cue to settle down. From now until the morning affirmation the wordcast would play quiet jazz and classical pieces.

Randdol considered bathing, or at least changing out of his clothes, but both seemed tiring and futile in equal measure. What was the point when in the morning he'd drag the same things onto his body?

Without even kicking off his shoes, he laid down on his bed, a single mattress tucked into the corner of the apartment. He closed his eyes, knowing sleep would come fast. Another benefit of living on the ninth floor: the exhaustion it brought on did wonders for his insomnia.

CHAPTER FOUR

Feeling stiff, Randdol took his time walking to work and ended up a few minutes late. When he stepped onto the floor of his office, the room was already lined from wall to wall with pasty men sitting at their oak desks.

The wordcast played the traditional heavy rock anthem that followed the morning affirmation at an increased volume. As a result, there was no office chatter or procrastination. Everyone sat at their computers getting about their work for the day.

Randdol eased into his chair. His lower back ached. He must have slept on it weird. Tonight, he would make sure he took a warm shower and changed out of his clothes.

Swiping his left hand across his desk, he activated his computer. The display bar glowed, and the screen solidified above it. He scrolled down, finding the daily briefing. It was best to read it first, so he knew what facts and stats he would work with throughout the day.

The briefing reported that The Word had fact-checked and discovered that the life expectancy rate in Hata had increased and that citizens were living longer, more fulfilled lives. Ten years ago, citizens were dying at the average age of fifty-eight, and now, thanks to the advancement and love of The Word, the average death rate was eighty-three.

Randdol groaned. The idea of living to eighty-three felt miserable. Better to be done with it then to drag it out. He knew not all the citizens of Hata felt as he did, and it was important for them to know the truth and facts. After all, that was why the scrubbers had been invented.

The scrubbers were damn good at their job. Randdol wasn't sure if they were pure algorithms or a working artificial intelligence, but either way they cleaned at an almost ninety-eight percent rate. Randol's job, and what all the other reporters did, was to double check for that extra two percent that the scrubbers missed.

The intranet was like the frontier, with no real laws or rules. It had an anything-goes mentality, and if it weren't for the scrubbers and reporters, the citizens would constantly face false information.

There was a kind of mind game to being a reporter, and Randdol enjoyed the puzzleyness of it. Knowing how the scrubbers worked, he could assume that they checked every website on the intranet and all social media to remove any references of someone dying before the age of eighty-three.

Randdol laughed because it only took him three minutes to figure out what the scrubbers had missed. The scrubbers had adjusted present day death records to show that the report from The Word was accurate, but they hadn't fixed the historical records from ten years ago.

Tweaking the parameters of a single scrubber, Randdol instructed it to adjust the death records over a ten-year time span, making sure the historical rates reflected what The Word had spoken.

He executed the scrubber and opened his queue to see what other issues needed fact-checked and scrubbed. He grew so engrossed with his work that at eleven when Banner tapped on his shoulder, it startled him.

Randdol hopped out of his chair, and the quick movement

brought a sharp stab to his lower back. "What the cack, Banner. Didn't you see I was working?"

"Lunch." Banner shrugged. The simple one-word answer explained everything.

Banner was right. The wordcast's volume had calmed and light chatter filled the office. The music would remain soft until the noon briefing, and then it would pick back up again after lunch.

Nodding, Randdol stretched and snatched his cane. "Let's get some grub. I'm starving."

Banner's chubby pale face shone with glee. Randdol had never met anyone who liked food cartridges more than Banner. It was how their whole friendship started. It was one of those days when the work cafeteria was serving pickled cod burgers. Randdol hated seafood, so he just ate the flatbread buns and was going to toss the rest of the lunch, but Banner stopped him to ask if he could have it.

Somehow that evolved into them being work friends, and on one level Randdol hated it because he wanted to be left alone, but no one else in the office liked Banner, as if they were scared he would eat their lunch, so by spending time with the cartridge connoisseur, it kept others away.

"You get anything big today?" Banner spoke a bit too loud, causing several other men on the lift to stare at him.

"Life expectancy issue," Randdol said. "Already cleared it. Didn't have a single thing to correct."

"That's good stuff. I never get good stuff." The lift stopped and Banner was the first one off and into the cafeteria. "All I got today were some printed pamphlets. I have to send the scrubbers to see if they can track down any online copies."

Banner held up a crudely made flier. Printed on it was a graffiti-style symbol. It resembled an eye, but its outer edges were cog-like blocks. Printed underneath it were the words "Resist Them."

Randdol whistled.

The symbol on the flier was the standard propaganda that The

Word used. There was nothing wrong with promoting it, but printed material was illegal.

Everything was digital because the scrubbers could only alter and control digital material. They could do nothing to correct lies printed in physical form. Getting a print case was the kind of job that bumped someone from being a junior reporter to a senior one. It seemed to be that idiots like Banner were always the ones that got the breaks while it was hard workers like himself who busted their butts and saw nothing for the effort.

～

The salty oyster pudding was so dry that it sucked the moisture from Randdol's tongue and clumped to the roof of his mouth. As disgusting as it was, he was happy it wasn't mashed peas stew.

Banner sat across the cafeteria table from him. The big man had finished his meal five minutes earlier, but was still using his fingers to scrape every morsel of the slimy pudding from his lunch cartridge. "Do you really think that would work?" Banner slurred his words while suckling on his pointer finger.

"I wouldn't have suggested it if I didn't," Randdol said.

"See that's why you are the best. You get reporting in a way that so many of us don't. I don't see why you're not promoted yet. You should be a senior reporter."

"Tell me about it." Randdol sighed and was about to clear away his cartridge, but stopped when the music of the wordcast dimmed.

"Good day citizens," The Word spoke in all of their heads. "Great news. The best news. A new study has been published showing that life expectancy has increased thanks to the safe environment The Word has created for you."

A round of applause filled the cafeteria.

"But we can't let this amazing news go to our heads," The Word continued. "We must be vigilant. The Opposition is near. The Opposition wants what you have, and only through resisting can we stop them."

Sharp whistles now broke through the clapping and cheering.

"Please take this time," The Word said. "And recommit yourselves."

As one, the cafeteria spoke, reciting the noontime prayer...

"The Word, hallowed is your voice. Be our protection against evils. Keep the wicked and damned at bay. Through the darkest of nights only your sound is true. Only you light the way. Only you give us the strength to resist them."

CHAPTER FIVE

Tayes shoved a whole butterbeer squash ravioli into her mouth. The stuffing was sweet and contrasted with the zesty pesto sauce. Getting real food had to be the best benefit of working in The White Tower. The food wasn't always as good, but it was better than the whack stuff in MicroPot cartridges.

The Brigade's cafeteria was so packed with brigaders that near the entrance some of the junior members were standing while they ate, but she sat alone. She wasn't offended. It was awkward to eat lunch with your boss.

The floor, the ceiling tiles, and even the tables in the round room were pure white. Well, almost. A spill from her meal left a green splotch. Using her sleeve, Tayes wiped away the green sauce that contrasted the white. She collected her tray and deposited her dirty dishes into a bin.

Intending to head back to her office, Tayes paused. Hobbes and an older, rounder black man stood by the entrance. She couldn't remember his name, but recognized him as one of the board members, the group responsible for Hata's budget.

The board member met Tayes' gaze and smiled. She cursed under her breath. There was no way she could sneak out now without greeting him.

In the center of the cafeteria, a group of recent brigaders academy graduates, most likely eighteen or nineteen years old, laughed as a pale boy dropped the bowl of ravioli into his upside-down helmet.

"I'm out." A brown girl sitting across from the boy rapped the table with her knuckles.

Those sitting around the pair jeered and laughed louder.

The boy squinted, as if trying to assume a street style attitude, and then picked up the helmet, placing it on his head. The helmet's rotors kicked in, closing around the boy's face.

The group counted out loud till five, and then the boy undid his helmet and slammed it on the table. His face was a gooey mess of pesto. Greasy globs of butterbeer squash ran down his neck and underneath his uniform.

"Pay up." The boy leaned over the table with his left arm out, palm up. "That's ten credit hours."

"Worth it." The girl laughed and held her left hand above his, with their tags almost touching.

Tayes had seen enough. She understood how stressful being in The Brigade could be and that brigaders needed some way to release steam, but she couldn't walk away from this. Too many people had observed her watching. She marched over.

"There are two things wrong with this situation." Tayes sat down next to the soggy boy.

The boy's eyes went wide, and he leaned back as if not believing them.

"If you name both things that are wrong," Tayes said, "and why they're wrong, I'll only write you up. If you can't, you and your friend will spend a month reassigned to the undercity. Does that sound fair?"

"Yes ma'am." No doubt, the boy meant it to sound strong, but it came out as a squeak.

"So, tell me," Tayes said. "Why am I ticked off?"

The boy wiped away a string of sauce running from his eyebrow to cheek. He blinked, and then his eyes focused down on the helmet. Smashed raviolis caked the smooth insides. "Because I wasted food."

"Excellent." Tayes clapped. "And the second reason?"

The boy looked to the girl who sat across from him.

She shrugged.

The boy sighed and shook his head. "Maybe because we caused you to stop and waste your time with us?"

"Nice." Tayes spoke in an overly warm tone. "Appealing to my ego. Quick thinking. And it almost worked, but unfortunately that's not the answer I was looking for."

The boy grimaced.

"Remind me, how important is that helmet of yours?" Tayes asked.

"Very important?"

"You asking or telling me?"

"Very important," he said.

"Your uniform and gear are not toys." Tayes shoved the helmet into the boy's chest. This is an advance tool that could save your life. You respect it or you will die. Understand?"

"Yes, ma'am!"

"Excellent," Tayes stood. "Tell your commander I want the both of you assigned to water filtration guard duty. If I check and you haven't done so, your punishment will be far worse."

"Yes, ma'am."

"As you were then." Tayes stepped away from the table, proud of herself. Assigning them to the undercity did a few things for Tayes. First, it was so dark down there that they would have to rely on their helmets. It would force them to realize how important their gear was. It also freed up two experienced brigaders that Hobbes had pulled off patrols and put them back on the streets. Even two bodies would help curb the current assault crises.

Scanning the crowd, Tayes hoped that Hobbes and the board

member had slipped out while she was busy. They hadn't. The two men still stood by the door and both were watching her with interest.

"What an honor to see the famous Catherine Tayes at work." The board member offered a hand to Tayes. "I'm Drake Weston."

"Pleasure, sir." Tayes shook his hand. "What are you doing here? I can't recall the last time I saw a city board member slumming it."

Drake Weston laughed.

"They are prepping for the annual budget and wanted to meet about the ratings." Hobbes scrunched his face as if trying to tell her something, but Tayes wasn't exactly sure what.

"Sounds horrible," Tayes said. "I think that's one of the best thing about working for Hobbes. He handles all of that mess so I can focus my attention on other matters, like keeping control of the city."

"If there is ever anything the board can do for a war hero like you," Weston said, "please let me know."

"Will do, sir," she said. "Now if you will excuse me, it's almost time for the evening affirmation. We do a shift change then, and I'd like to see the night crew as they head out."

"Of course," Weston said. "You do good work here. All of us at the board have noticed."

"Thank you, sir." Tayes smiled. Not a real one, but the polite kind you give to a stranger.

Hobbes glared at Tayes, and she wondered if she had said or done something wrong. By his look, she had, but she didn't understand what. Ultimately, it wasn't her problem. The budget, ratings, the board—those were the only things that Hobbes had to deal with. If things weren't going well, then it was up to him to fix it. She was too busy trying to keep the city at peace to worry about such nonsense.

CHAPTER SIX

An hour before the end of his work day, a new item appeared in Randdol's queue. It was a report from The Brigade, stating that criminal assaults were down and that there hadn't been an assault in Hata in over ten weeks.

Leaning back from his work desk, Randdol grimaced. That couldn't be right when the night before he'd seen the connivance store employee arrested for assault.

Randdol reread the report to make sure he hadn't misinterpreted. It stated there hadn't been a murder in years and that the last assault took place ten weeks ago. He knew without a doubt that the report was false.

These kinds of glitches happened now and then, though off the top of his head he couldn't remember a specific one. Not wanting to get in trouble for failing to clear his queue, Randdol summoned a scrubber. He tweaked its parameters and executed.

An alert box appeared on his screen, reporting that the scrubber had successfully finished its job.

Returning to his queue, he reread the top item. He was shocked to see it still said the last assault had happened ten weeks ago. Assaults in Hata were rare. The city was a place where everyone could feel safe. Just the idea of an assault happening not that long ago was scary. He himself had been lucky. Not since the war had he seen an assault in person. Sure, there were the holovids, but everyone knew those weren't real.

Not finding any deviations in the scrubbers, Randdol marked the item as complete. It was the last item on his to-do list, and it always made him feel relieved to see his queue empty. It meant that it was time to head home. With a wave of his hand, he shut down his computer, and scooped up his cane.

While waiting for the lift, the wordcast shifted from music to its evening report. The Word thanked the citizens for working hard all day and it congratulated those working late shifts on earning the extra credit hours.

The Word then announced that the evening entertainment was The Boy and the Rat. A smile crept across his lips. Most days, Randdol ignored the evening tales, having heard each dozens of time, but The Boy and the Rat was his favorite.

∼

The Boy had no name. He was simply The Boy. And the world he lived in was one of terror. This was before the dawning of The Word, back in the dark ages where people went hungry, and rape and murder were everyday fears.

The Boy lived in the inner city, a slum-like-place where few children lived to be teenagers. The Boy's mother had died addicted to drugs and his father was an alcoholic who lived on the charity of others, never working a day in his life.

The Boy saw the wickedness in his father's way, and before the age of ten he would do jobs around the slum. On a good day, he would make enough money to buy bread and jam. On the bad days, he went hungry.

In the summer, back when there were still seasons, the days were longer, and one night when he was out late, The Boy came upon a group of thugs, hoodlums with clothes too big. They had anger in their eyes as they threw stones into an alley.

A rock the size of a fist struck something in the shadows. There was a screeching sound, and the thugs scattered. The Boy, too curious for his own good, decided to see what the thugs had been doing. The Boy found a dog hiding in the heaps of garbage. It was shaggy, with fur so matted that it could hardly move. Its ribs were visible and its paws covered in chew marks.

"You are dirty and gross," The Boy said. "Like a rat."

The name, Rat, stuck and because The Boy had a heart too big for his own good, he took Rat home, splitting the bread and jam he had earned that day.

The seasons passed and after much scrubbing, cleaning, and care, Rat became The Boy's best friend. They always shared their food and went about the inner city together, working and playing.

The next winter was the start of The Broken War. The Opposition came with their radicalized ways, and they rained terror upon the cities, including the one where The Boy and Rat lived. Chemicals suffocated the inner city, with green mists flooding the streets, squeezing through the cracks in the buildings and driving the residents mad.

Locked in their shanty, with walls as thin as aluminum, The Boy feared death. On the streets, mad men and females attacked anything that moved, going so far as to eat the faces off each other.

The Boy's father, who usually passed out drunk by late afternoon, had gone through his liquor supply quicker than normal and instead of being home sleeping, he had been on the streets as the mist fell. Like a rampaging baboon, he returned home, and with brute inhuman strength, he ripped down the walls to their shack.

The boy screamed and picked up a brick, clenching it in his fist as his only weapon. But Rat acted first, leaping at The Boy's father. The dog's canines bit into the man's throat, while its claws dug and scratched at the man's face.

Blood gushed from the wounds and The Boy's father fell. For a moment, The Boy thought they were safe, but then his father stirred. In a quick twist, the man snapped Rat's neck and discarded the dog's body as if it were no more than a dirty piece of clothing.

The Boy's father lunged at his son, pinning the child to the rotted wooden floor of the shack. Swinging his brick, The Boy tried to fight off the attack, but he wasn't strong enough. Completely lost to the toxins, The Boy's father extended his jaw, preparing to eat The Boy's face.

With the last bit of his strength, The Boy kicked, jamming his heel over and over again into his father's nose and cheek. The Boy's father caught the foot. The mad creature bit down, severing The Boy's big toe and part of his pointer toe.

Hot pain rushed across The Boy's body. He screamed, and in one last ditch effort, he swung the brick, bashing it against his father's temple. The corner of the brick dug in deep.

The Boy's father went limp, his weight pinning The Boy to the floor. In the chaos and terror, no one came for The Boy. It took sixteen hours, but the boy clawed his way out from under his father's corpse.

Woozy and weak, The Boy took the time to spit on his father's dead body, happy the man was gone.

∼

Randdol knew the spin that The Word put on the story. If The Boy hadn't wasted so much of his food and energy caring for Rat, then when his father had attacked him, he would have been strong enough to defend himself.

That was not how Randdol saw the story. To him it was a tragedy of love. The Boy had loved Rat and Rat loved The Boy. It proved that no matter how foul and dark the world got, unconditional love could not be destroyed.

Letting out a yawn, Randdol looked up from the road. He'd spent most of the walk home on autopilot, listening to the story. Now he stood in front of a connivance store. He didn't know why, but something nagged at him that the store was important. Something in the back of his mind told him this, and yet he had no idea what it could be.

The sensible thing to do would be to go home, have his food cartridge, and settle down for the night, but his gut told him that was a mistake. Without giving it much more thought, Randdol crossed the street for the connivance store's door.

CHAPTER SEVEN

As Randdol approached the connivance store, he couldn't keep his eyes off the woman who stood in its window. She was in her late forties and garbed in a slimming red dress. It had lace around her cleavage and a floral pattern on the bottom trim. Maybe if she were twenty years younger, she would do well for herself, but she was a sad sight to see.

A digital bell chimed above Randdol's head as he entered the store. The shop was laid out in a u-shape with a divider separating a lobby area from the main parlor. The lobby had several bookshelves lined with adult toys, and lime green faded walls that hadn't been painted or kept up in decades.

Waiting for Randdol in the parlor was the woman from the window. She had stepped off her stage and leaned against a marsala-colored high-backed chair. She stood with intention, her breasts out, as if they were calling to him.

"How can I service you?" she asked in a silky voice as if she already knew the answer.

"I got a bit of credit hours to spare," Randdol said. "Thought I might put them to good use."

At the mention of credit hours, the woman's posture changed. She shifted her weight and slid over the arm of the chair, so she draped across it. "I'm the only one on shift, right now. I'd be happy to service you."

The back of the parlor had three doors. Between the doors were ottomans, all of which were equally drab. Two were ripped, and the third wore red stains on its side. Randdol guessed the rooms were where the ladies did their work. "Where are the other clerks?"

"Something you don't like about me?" The woman ran a hand along her neck, drawing Randdol's eyes toward her breasts.

"No." Randdol looked around the room. He still wasn't sure why he was here, just that something felt wrong. "Just seems odd to only have one clerk on shift at a time."

"Aggie was supposed to work tonight, but no one has seen her since last night. Were you one of her regulars?"

"No, just wondering. What's your name?"

"Evelyn." Her voice slid into a sultry tone. "You want to play?"

"I think I'm all right." Randdol raised his cane as if making a toast. "Thank you."

"Let me know if you change your mind."

The bell to the store chimed, and a bulky man stepped from the lobby and into the parlor. The man reeked of onions. He bumped into Randdol, almost knocking him over with his body and his smell.

"You can't be here." Evelyn sat up, putting her arms across her chest. "Get out or I'll call in The Brigade for non-payment."

"That's why I'm here." The man held out his left hand. "I'm settling up on my credit hours."

Evelyn held out her left hand. "Then do it."

Instead of lining up his tag with Evelyn's, the onion man grabbed her wrist and pulled her to her feet. "I'll pay, but after."

Randdol knew this wasn't his business. Everyone had their work to do, and it wasn't his place to get involved. Getting involved was dangerous. Both in the moment and later with the possibility of being exported to a labor city. Every instinct in Randdol's body told him to walk out the door and not look back, but there was something about Evelyn that ground him in place.

"Buddy." Randdol thudded his cane on the floor. "Get in line. I was here first."

"Piss off," the onion man said.

Randdol crossed to the high-back chair and sat down. Using his cane, he tapped out the beat of the music playing on the wordcast.

"You stupid?" The onion man let go of Evelyn and took a step toward Randdol. "I told you to piss off!"

Randdol continued to tap along with the music.

"You some sick pervert who likes to watch then?" The onion man recoiled. "I should beat some sense into you."

Randdol blinked once. Then twice. "Sorry," he said. "I zone out sometimes. Did you say something?"

"That's it." The onion man stood so close that Randdol was eye level with the man's crotch. "Get out now."

"What is that?" Randdol sniffed the air and then winced in a melodramatic manner, trying to oversell the point. "Does your dick always stink like that or did you literally make love to an onion?

The onion man's nostrils flared. Red flowed across his face.

"For starters, where did you even get an onion?" Randdol laid his hands across his cane. "I've not seen one in years."

The onion man clenched his hand into a fist.

"And to follow that up," Randdol said. "How did you make love to it? Was it a big onion or do you just have a small prick?"

The onion man cocked his arm back as if to strike Randdol.

Randdol screamed and threw his hands into the air. Kicking off the floor, he flipped the high chair backwards. "You hit me!"

"I did no such thing!" The onion man stepped away, showing both his palms.

"The camera is right behind you," Randdol said. "I'm sure it captured the whole thing."

The three-sixty-degree camera hung in the window of the connivance store. If Randdol had done his job right, the footage should make it look like the onion man had committed some sort of assault.

"She's just a whore," the onion man said. "Why do you even care?"

"I just do." Randdol rolled out of the fallen chair, his back screaming in pain. "Now get out and don't come back. There are plenty of other connivance stores you can visit. Find another one."

"You both are cack!" The onion man pumped a fist into the air. He snatched an ottoman and threw it across the room. In the lobby, he flipped one of the bookshelves and delivered a hard kick to the wall, his boot crashing through the rotted wood.

The onion man gave a final yell and burst out of the store.

"That wasn't necessary." Evelyn righted the high-back chair.

"I know," Randdol said. "But it was the right thing to do."

"It wasn't. You put us both at risk."

"So, what was I supposed to do?"

"Let me do my job and make a living."

"Okay then," Randdol said. "Then I guess I'll be going."

"So, that's two customers I lose tonight?"

Randdol didn't know if she was propositioning him for service or if she was demanding a credit-hour payment in retribution for what she would have made. "I'm not really in the mood."

Evelyn hooked her arm into his, guiding him to a door at the back of the parlor. Chunky veins lined the tops of her hands and the number of age spots suggested that at some point she'd spent a lot of time in the sun.

Now Randdol was certainly not in the mood. Slipping free from her grasp, he spun to face the lobby. A twinkling light caught his attention.

Splintered wood blocked most of the hole that the onion man kicked in the wall, and yet, as Randdol stared at it, he could make out a glowing azure light coming from the other side.

CHAPTER EIGHT

An hour after the evening affirmation played, Randdol and Evelyn had finished enlarging the hole in the wall so they could fit through. On the other side was a half-flight of stairs that led down to a brick room.

Heat-emitting azure lights were crudely hung from the ceiling. The thick air felt wet against Randdol's exposed skin. There was also a musky smell as if it hadn't been vented in years.

"Oh, my word!" Evelyn gasped.

Three mounds of green brambles stretched under the lights. The vines created tangles that hid the entire floor.

"What is this place?" Evelyn asked.

"It's a grow room," Randdol said.

The last grow room Randdol had seen was for carrots. That had been back when Hata switched to MicroPot cartridges. Growing food became illegal because the energy and water was deemed better spent on more important things. The citizens didn't take to the new law and grow rooms sprouted across the city while those with power or influence could create gardens that authorities ignored.

For these plants to have flourished so well, there must be a water source close by. Near the center of the room, Randdol spotted a sprinkler with a digital device attached to it. He guessed the device had a timer of some sort. With healthy soil and water, there was no telling how long this room had been hidden, but it was clear from the chaotic growth that no one had checked on it for a long time.

"Those are berries, aren't they?" Evelyn stood almost engulfed in one of the mounds. Her knuckles brushed a bramble, and she yelped, retracting her arm. "That smarts."

The berries were plump and bumpy on the outside. They looked like a bunch of bubbles that had been smashed together. A sharp, sweet smell rose from them. Randdol couldn't quite remember the name of the plant.

"Raspberries." Evelyn rubbed away a dot of blood from the back of her hand. "That's what they're called. Be careful. The thorns are sharp."

Evelyn made another grab for a berry, this time plucking it free and popping the whole thing in her mouth. She closed her eyes. The lines on her face relaxed, and she made a humming sound.

"That good, eh?" Randdol asked.

"Better than you can imagine."

Using his cane to bat away the loose brambles, Randdol scooted closer to the heart of the bush and freed his own berry. Dropping the raspberry onto his tongue, he smashed it against the roof of his mouth. A sweet, tangy juice splurged forth and ran down his throat. He couldn't remember ever eating anything so sweet and delicate.

"This has to be our secret." Evelyn didn't so much as suggest it as she commanded it. "This is a treasure and if The Brigade found out…"

She didn't have to say. He knew what would happen. The whole building would be burned and both of them exported.

"We can't trust anyone else." Evelyn waved a berry under her nose. "A secret like this would be impossible to keep. If we told anyone, then word would spread. You must promise not to tell."

"I have no one to tell." He meant it as truth. No one in his life was worth a secret like this. "Can I trust you not to tell your coworkers?"

Crossing through the brambles, like a goddess floating on water, she made her way to his side. She took the berry she had been smelling and plopped it into his mouth. "This is only for you and me."

Her breath smelled of raspberries, and a trail of juice ran from her lush lips. He imagined how soft they would feel against his own. He wondered what she tasted like. Could he taste her over the sweet tartness of the berries?

"Our secret," he said in a low voice. His heart beat faster. He wanted her. He wanted her to be his. He didn't care how old she was. There was still a beauty in her, a raw sexiness that couldn't be quenched. He didn't care how many credit hours he had to spend—he would make it happen.

She kissed him on his jawbone, near the ear. A tingling sensation ran across his skin as goosebumps flared down his neck.

"Thank you. For before," she said. "For upstairs."

Randdol couldn't muster words. His thoughts were lost, lingering on what her naked body might look like.

Evelyn pulled away from him and looked to the half-flight of stairs. "My shift ends soon. We need to have that hole covered before one of the late-night clerks gets in."

Reality snapped back in place for Randdol. She was right. There would be plenty of time for him to indulge himself. The highest priority was to protect their secret.

A rusted sheet of metal sat in the back corner of the room. Roughly three feet wide and four feet tall, it looked about the right size to cover the hole in the wall.

Randdol moved toward the sheet of metal. Halfway to it, his cane sunk, as if being sucked into the floor. Without the support, he fell, crashing into a nest of brambles. Thorns dug into his knees and shins while the metallic taste of blood drowned out any lingering raspberry juice that remained in his mouth.

"By The Word!" Evelyn rushed to his side. "Are you all right?"

"I've been through worse." Letting Evelyn pull him to his feet, he looked around confused, unsure of what had happened. From what he could tell, it was as if one second there was floor and in the next there was none.

All Randdol could see of his cane was the handle sticking three inches above the vines. He cleared away the surrounding brambles and discovered a metal grate, two feet by three feet wide. It must be where the water drained when the sprinkler system kicked in. He was a fool for not thinking to check for something like that. He had to be more careful.

"Where do you think it goes?" Evelyn asked.

"No idea," he said. "But it should be the only one. I'll be fine now."

Maroon blossoms stained his pant legs and his white button-up shirt. It was a shame because he only had two work outfits, but considering what he was gaining with the raspberries, he supposed a few random bits of clothing were meaningless.

Still tasting blood, he ran a finger across his lips, but they seemed fine, so he felt around the inside of his mouth with his tongue.

"What is it?" Evelyn asked.

"I think I cracked a tooth." Randdol's gum was tender, and he felt a distinct ridge along the side of his right back tooth. Grasping her hand, he gave it a slight squeeze. "It's all right. I'll be fine, but we should hurry. I want to make sure our secret stays secret."

CHAPTER NINE

Tayes settled down in her apartment when the private cast came in. She heard a solid tone and then a voice spoke. "Assistant Warden? Ma'am?"

Tayes pinched her tag. "What is it?"

"Problem with one of the citizens."

"Which?"

"Randdol Mupt, ma'am."

"What's the situation?" Tayes stripped out of a plain white tank top and retrieved her work uniform form her dirty clothing pile. She had taken it off less than ten minutes ago, but she still gave it a sniff test before putting it back on.

"We lost him."

"You can't lose him." Tayes scooted into her work pants and strapped on her armored equipment belt. "That can't be right."

"We did."

"You need to give me more than that." Tayes scooped her helmet off its rack and snapped it on.

"The tracker says he's at a connivance store—"

"The one from last night?"

"Yes."

"And you don't see him on the camera feed?"

"No, but the furniture is overturned, like there was some sort of altercation."

"Hold on." Tayes waved a hand, locking her apartment door behind her as she ran to the lift. "I'll be there in less than a minute, and we can check the hidden set of cameras."

For the umpteenth time, Tayes was glad that The Brigade had implemented a hidden camera system throughout Hata. Most everyone knew The Brigade was always watching. There was no denying that. So instead, The Brigade hung a flag on it. All public spaces had a large, oversized camera impossible to miss. When citizens didn't see one of them, they assumed they were safe. They weren't.

Mind you, the secret cameras weren't perfect. There were still a few blind-spots in the city, a nook here or a space behind a doorway. But it was amazing the footage The Brigade captured just because people assumed no one was watching.

The doors to the lift opened, and Tayes entered a room filled with glass cubicles. Each station had their own tech, and she had no idea which of the techs was the one she had spoken to.

Tayes cupped her hands around her mouth. "Who called me?"

The room went still.

A female tech wearing the standard plain whites and blues of staff employees waved a hand from halfway down the room.

Making a beeline to the station, Tayes ignored the buzz as everyone continued to watch her. "What's your name?"

"Amber," the tech said.

"All right, Amber, show me the last footage you have."

Amber brought up two screens. On the first was a graph with vital signs. In the second was a holovid. "I first became aware something was off when I saw a spike in Randdol Mupt's vitals. Not the usual spike we see from those in the connivance store. This was pain, but when I tried to find him on camera, I couldn't."

The vid played back at triple speed. Shot from inside the parlor of the connivance store: it showed Randdol entering. Another man soon followed. There seemed to be an argument. The other man got physical and then left.

"Rewind till where the man knocked over the chair," Tayes said. "I didn't notice a spike in pain for Randdol."

Amber rewound and replayed the altercation in real time. As Tayes had noted, Randdol's vitals for pain showed no spikes.

"Show me the rest," Tayes said.

The vid played, showing Randdol talking to the clerk. That lasted a few minutes, and then they both seemed to disappear off camera as if they were leaving. Amber switched to an exterior shot of the building, but at no point did Randdol exit.

Tayes waved her hand across the floor. Her tag pinged. "Your station is authorized to handle the classified system. Bring up another camera from inside the store."

Amber twisted around the controls. Three more holovids opened. Two were from the back rooms and showed nothing but empty beds. The third was from the right side of the parlor.

The new vids played at an accelerated speed, and Amber slowed them down when their time code matched the altercation.

"And there it is," Tayes said.

The vid showed Randdol kicking over his own chair while the big man watched in confusion.

"Balling," Amber swore. "That's some hardcore sneaky cack."

Tayes agreed, but she wasn't surprised.

The vid continued until Randdol and the clerk disappeared behind the partition separating the lobby and parlor.

"Do we not have another camera in there?" Tayes asked.

"The partition is new, less than a year old. I don't think until now anyone realized it blocked our view of the room."

"What do you think? Five to six feet of dead space that we don't have covered?"

Amber brought up the technical specs for the building. "Looks to be a bit more. The space is about eight feet by six feet."

"Contact dispatch," Tayes said. "Send a team after him."

A blip on one of the holovids jittered.

"Hold on, ma'am," Amber said. "He's on the move."

Amber minimized all the holovids and went to a live feed. It showed Randdol exiting the store.

Tayes examined Randdol's vitals graph. His pain levels were still higher than where they should be. "This seem right to you?"

"It could be chronic pain." Amber squinted at the vid as if trying to pick it apart. "Let me compare this to his historical data."

A second graph popped into the air next to the first. Amber twisted her hands together and the two graphs overlaid each other. "It's clear his present pain levels are double what they should be."

"He's hurt and something funky happened," Tayes said. "Get me an ETA on the team. I want him brought in now!"

CHAPTER TEN

Never in Randdol's life had the walk up nine flights of stairs been easier. They blinked by, with his mind thinking about Evelyn.

After blocking the hole in the wall with the metal sheet, they'd rearranged all the bookshelves in the connivance store, moving them to cover the busted wall. He felt confident they were in the clear, and he was sure they'd have a future together.

The door to his apartment auto-opened and the kitchen light kicked on. For half a second, he thought about eating his steak patty food cartridge, but today was already special. No need to do any extra celebrating.

Deciding to skip dinner, he stripped out of his bloodstained clothes and made his way to the bathroom. The cuts on his arm weren't deep, but blue bruises were forming around them. His knees and shins were another story all together.

When he fell in the cellar, he must have bounced or slid because instead of small holes, he had streaking cuts. Some were still oozing with blood. At a younger age they would have been a minor bother, something he would shrug off, but now, an untreated infection could lead to serious consequences.

Climbing into his shower pod, he set the pressure and heat for higher than normal. It would hurt, but sanitation was more important than pain.

As the pod hummed, readying to mist Randdol, a crash ripped through the apartment. Wood splintering. Glass shattering. Boots clambering.

Before Randdol could see who or what made the sound, he knew. The Brigade had come for him.

The door to the shower pod flew open.

Bright lights shined in Randdol's eyes. He couldn't see how many there were.

A stinging pain, like that of a wasp, struck his naked chest. He glanced down in time to see electricity arcing across his skin.

∼

Randdol sat on a white sandy beach. The waters surrounding it were a crystal blue and beside him sat a dog. He didn't know enough about dogs to know what kind it was. It was short and stubby, with floppy ears and curly brown fur that covered its heft.

"I love you," the dog said.

"You can talk?" Randdol asked.

"I've always talked. Now is just the first time you're listening."

That made sense to Randdol. He didn't know how, but he knew the dog was right. "You're Rat."

"I am."

"Where are we?"

"Wrong question."

Randdol slapped himself in the forehead. Rat was right. That was a stupid question. They were sitting on a beach. That was obvious. The sun was high, and its light felt warm on his naked skin. In the distance, he could hear gulls and the lulling peace of the crashing waves.

"Sensors were right," a voice said. "Cracked tooth."

Randdol spun, trying to see who'd spoken.

Twenty feet behind him was a tropical forest, with huge coconut trees and massive vines that would be perfect for swinging on, but he didn't see any animals. The beach, in both directions, was also deserted.

"Who said that?" Randdol looked down at Rat.

"A better question."

"And?"

Rat used his muzzle and nudged Randdol's hand upward.

The sky was dark, like night, but there was a crack, like a window, cutting through it. On the other side of the floating window he could see movement, but everything was out of focus.

"He damaged the transmitter chip in the molar," a second voice said.

"That's why there's a back-up." The first voice sounded annoyed, like a parent talking to a child.

"Has this happened before?" the second voice asked.

"With him?" the first voice said. "No, but it's not uncommon. That's why we implanted the back-ups."

Randdol ran a hand along his jaw. He could feel a warm sensation. It wasn't pain, more like the warmth of a heating pad. These voices were clearly talking about him and his teeth.

Crouching to eye level with Rat, Randdol rubbed the dog behind his ear, knowing it was Rat's favorite place to be scratched. "How do I see who is talking? I need to know what is happening."

"That's the right question." Rat stretched and curved his body, so that Randdol's scratching ran down the dog's spine. "Open your eyes."

The concept of opening one's eyes seemed simple to Randdol, but he wasn't sure what Rat meant. "They are open." Randdol waved a hand in front of his face. It moved so fast that his fingers blurred together in wavy lines.

"Not those eyes," Rat said. "Your real eyes."

Randdol still didn't get what Rat was talking about, but if his eyes were open, then he assumed he must close them before he could open them again. So, he did. In the darkness he could still hear Rat's breathing, but the sound of the waves crashing and the winds stirring the trees faded. In their place, he heard rubber shoes scuffing a freshly buffed floor and the sound of electronic equipment beeping.

With all his might, Randdol opened his eyes. Cracks split in the darkness, and he saw two men with surgical masks covering their faces. They both wore scrubs, and they seemed to be in a bright white room.

Randdol noticed a horrible dryness in his mouth. He couldn't feel his lips, tongue, or cheeks, but he could tell that his mouth was dry as if he had eaten a mouthful of the white sand. He tried to close his mouth, but something inside held it open.

Looking for a reflection of himself, his gaze fell upon a pair of x-rays. They were full scans of his mouth, showing three crowns and two filled cavities. The x-rays looked almost normal except his back two molars. Something was wrong with them. The right molar had a crack in it, and both the right and left had a black square inside the white of the x-ray.

One man in scrubs held a pair of tweezers. Pinched between the tips was Randdol's cracked tooth. The man pried open the crack with a hook-like device, revealing a microchip. "Wow," the second voice said. "He really tore it up."

"I've seen worse," said the other man.

The second man cocked his head sideways and looked into Randdol's eyes. "He's waking up."

"Give him a double dose this time. That should do it."

The man with the tooth turned a dial on a machine behind him. The second it happened, Randdol's eyelids grew heavy. He tried not to shut them, but it was as if they had a will of their own.

Randdol blinked, and when he did, he found himself back on the white beach with Rat.

"Did you find what you were looking for?" Rat lay with his feet up in the air and wiggled as if trying to use the sand to scratch a spot on his back.

"No," Randdol said. "I found something worse."

CHAPTER ELEVEN

The morning wordcast upped its volume, waking Randdol. He lay in his bed and rolled over, confused, unsure of what was a dream, what was real, and if he really was at home. At last he decided the music, some awful rock medley with gnashing guitars and quick drums, was too horrible for him to create in a dream. This had to be real.

Weak, as if the muscles in his legs had shrunk, he went to the bathroom. He inspected himself in the mirror, intending to check out his teeth, but froze. The cuts on his arms were gone. So were the worst ones on his legs.

Did the Brigade use some sort of healing apparatus on him? Had he been kept unconscious for such a long time that his wounds healed? Or, had he just imagined the whole thing?

Opening his mouth, he saw he had both his back molars, and neither was cracked. That didn't confirm or deny his memories. The only way he could prove what he remembered was real would be talking to Evelyn.

He always needed the credit hours, so skipping work wasn't an option, but the second he got off, he would visit Evelyn and tell her everything he'd seen.

The music of the wordcast quieted, and The Word began the morning affirmation. "Resist them. Trust The Word. The Word will not lie. It is loyal to you. It wants you great. It wants you safe from The Opposition. The Opposition wants to take. They want your freedom. They want your thoughts. They want you. The Opposition will come. When it does, resist them."

Usually by the time the affirmation started, Randdol was almost to work. That meant he was at least a half hour off schedule, which could get him in deep trouble if he didn't hurry.

Randdol slipped into a pair of charcoal-colored pants and a white shirt, but once more was surprised when he saw his closet had two additional pairs of the same outfit. Something was not right. He had never owned three pairs of work clothes. The Brigade had done something to him.

The music of the wordcast shifted, and Randdol kicked into gear. He couldn't run, but he moved as fast as he was capable. He got to work in the nick of time and threw himself into his chair, his chest heaving.

The queue for the day ended up being small, and he finished his work by noon. Instead of doing the usual lunch with Banner, he skipped out to go see Evelyn.

The bell to the connivance store chimed as he entered, and he was pleased to see the bookshelves were still blocking the hole in the wall. The fact that they had been moved was proof that his memories were real.

"Want to party?" a woman with a deep voice said. She stood in the parlor entrance. She was on the hefty side and definitely not Evelyn.

"I'm here to see Evelyn," Randdol said. "I'm a regular."

The woman's face sank. "Sorry to be the one to tell you, but she's gone."

"Gone?"

The woman pointed out the store's front window. Looming over the building across the street stood The White Tower.

Randdol felt like someone had punched him. It was hard to breathe, and he felt light headed. "When... when did it happen?"

"Ten days ago, maybe twelve," the woman said. "Something like that."

That confirmed his other suspicion. He'd been a prisoner of The Brigade for at least two weeks. Why had they taken Evelyn? Had she known at the time that they had him? Did she think he'd betrayed her to them? If they brought him back, would they do the same for her? That seemed strange. Randdol couldn't think of any other citizen who had ever returned after being taken in by The Brigade.

"I know it's a shame to lose your favorite clerk, I'd be happy to charge you half the credit hours." The chunky woman ran her sausage-like fingers across her waist.

Randdol wanted to hurl.

He left the connivance store. The prostitute called something out at him, but he didn't hear what. His mind focused on Evelyn. He could picture her lips and the way she smiled when she ate her first raspberry. He could hear her soft voice and feel her lips on his neck.

Only a memory. She was gone. The only bright thing he had in this world was gone.

The days blurred.

He woke. The clock struck 8:01.

"Resist them. Trust The Word. The Word will not lie. It is loyal to you. It wants you great. It wants you safe from The Opposition. The Opposition wants to take. They want your freedom. They want your thoughts. They want you. The Opposition will come. When it does, resist them."

Work. Lunch.

"The Word, hallowed is your voice. Be our protection against evils. Keep the wicked and damned at bay. Through the darkest of nights only your sound is true. Only you light the way. Only you give us the strength to resist them."

Home. Mashed peas stew.

The clock struck 8:01.

"Resist them. Trust The Word. The Word will not lie. It is loyal to you. It wants you great. It wants you safe from The Opposition. The Opposition wants to take. They want your freedom. They want your thoughts. They want you. The Opposition will come. When it does, resist them."

Sleep.

Over and over again.

And again, and again, and again.

The days were the same. The only glimpse he ever had of hope was on his walk home. He always passed the connivance store and always took the time to look through the window for Evelyn.

She was never there.

Randdol lost track of the days. Each being a not-exact perfect copy of the one before it. Existing like this was the opposite of living. It was hell. Dying would be better than repeating the endless cycle of days where nothing changed. Especially when he knew at all times The Brigade was watching. They were in his teeth. They had their cameras and would never let him be.

"Hear about the guy in food distribution?"

"What?" Randdol shook his head and processed that he was at his work cafeteria, eating lunch with Banner.

"The guy in food distribution." Banner reached across the table and took Randdol's food cartridge. Randdol didn't bother objecting. "Turns out he was in love with another guy. Something happened, I don't know what, and the guy he was in love with got sent to one of the labor cities. So, the guy in food distribution when bat crazy. He decided he wanted to be taken too, so do you know what he did?"

Randdol shook his head.

"He cacked on his desk."

"You're joking."

"I cack you not!" Banner laughed and slammed his palm on the table. "I saw it as The Brigade was dragging him out. It was runny."

"Didn't need to know that last bit."

"I think it's relevant." Banner held the food cartridge up to his mouth and slurped whatever the brown mush was out of it. "It's how you know the story is real. With a detail like that it can't be made up."

"Do you think it worked? Do you think the guy ended up being sent to the same labor city?"

"Hell if I know, but I think you're missing the point of the story."

"What?"

"That he cacked on his desk!" Banner laughed again.

Randdol was fascinated by the food distribution guy getting himself turned in. Something like that had never occurred to Randdol before now. If he broke the law and pissed off The Brigade, would they send him to the same labor city they hauled Evelyn off to? He had no way to know, and as an old man, he wouldn't last more than a week in one of those cities.

And yet, he couldn't let the idea go. The food distribution guy had decided he wanted something, and he went for it. It was stupid and surely didn't work out in his favor, but he had the balls to go after it. No one that Randdol could think of had ever stood up to The Brigade.

As much as he wanted Evelyn, dying for her wasn't worth it, but sticking it to The Brigade could be. He just had to figure out how he could do that.

Banner tapped Randdol and then pointed at his temple. "You aren't saying it."

The noontime prayer was playing across the wordcast and Randdol hadn't noticed. He mouthed "thanks" to Banner and joined in with the last bit of the prayer.

"Only you light the way. Only you give us the strength to resist them."

The words spoke to Randdol in a way they never had. They shined on the one weakness of The Brigade. To them, The Word was law. It was the one thing they treasured. If Randdol wanted to hurt them, the best way to do it would be to hurt The Word.

CHAPTER TWELVE

Tayes put a hand on Hobbes' office door, intending to pull it open, but stopped upon hearing Barbra inside. Barbra was using the tone she usually reserved for subordinates. It was the bubbly-grandma tone mixed with a hint of her why-are-you-so-stupid tone. If Barbra was busting it out on Hobbes it meant that Hobbes had seriously stuck his foot in his mouth.

"Do you have a better idea on how to handle the tech shift schedule without them accruing overtime and without new hires?" Barbra paused as if to let her words sink in. "If not then I'll do what I think is right and if any of those from the hundredth floor have a problem you can send them to me."

Barbra's heels clicked on the floor and Tayes backed away, not wanting to be caught eavesdropping.

The door swung open and Barbra made eye contact with Tayes. Tayes raised a brow. Barbra touched the side of her nose.

"What?" Tayes mouthed.

Barbra leaned in close. "I think he's back on eldar juice."

That was news to Tayes. She hadn't realized Hobbes had

ever been on the substance. Of course, she wasn't into the office gossip in the ways that Barbra was. Eldar juice was forbidden and yet dirt cheap. It was an upper that enhanced with one's memory. In small doses it could be used for medicinal purposes, but if abused it could distort one's reality. "How do you know?" Tayes asked.

"Just watch," Barbra said. "I'm sure you'll notice."

Tayes nodded. She knew the signs. Paranoia, uncontrolled outbursts, and chronal dysplasia were the biggest and yet anyone stuck working in Hata for an extended period of time could easily appear to be suffering from all three. But that didn't mean Barbra was wrong. Tayes would have to keep an eye on Hobbes.

"Stop by my office when you're done," Barbra said.

"You brought pie for lunch?" Tayes smiled at the thought of Barbra's homemade pecan ginger pies.

"No, I just figured you'd need to vent."

"Will do." Tayes waved goodbye and entered Hobbes' office, shutting the door behind her.

Hobbes looked up from paperwork, wearing a scowl. "I called you in over an hour ago," he said.

"Was in the city."

"Sit."

Tayes did as she was told.

"I want to know why you're here," Hobbes said.

"You ordered me here."

He licked his lips and looked down at his desk. "That's not what I meant and you know it."

"I don't know what you mean." For once she wasn't playing coy or messing with him.

"Why are you here in Hata? Why are you still doing this job? You're a war hero. You could be practically anywhere and living a cushy life."

She knew this was coming. It always seemed to crop up with her superiors. Hobbes had brought her in to talk because he felt threatened. "I'm good at what I do, and for me, this city is of particular interest."

"Because you grew up in Old Hata?" There was a tone as if he were trying to use that against her.

"No, it's not sentimentalism," she said. "It's more duty. I'm here because I don't trust anyone else to do the job we do."

"I don't buy that." He formed his hands into a pyramid shape. He had done it ever since he attended a leadership seminar last season. As if for some bullcack reason forming a pyramid with one's hands could make someone more intimidating. "Not two weeks ago you were saying things to Drake Weston."

"The board member?"

"Don't play dumb. That day in the cafeteria was some of the best stunt work I've ever seen."

Tayes leaned back in her chair. "What the cack are you talking about?"

"Your run-in with the academy graduates. You made a big show and speech. It was obvious you were doing it all for Weston's sake."

"I was doing my duty as Assistant Warden."

"Bull." Hobbes dropped his pyramid and crossed his arm. "Admit it. You were trying to impress Weston!"

"Why would I care about what a board member thinks of me? I don't give a rat's ass about what happens on the higher levels of The White Tower or what happens outside of this city." Tayes pointed at Hobbes and then back at herself. "That's how this works. You deal with that crap. All I care about is Hata."

"What if our arrangement isn't good enough anymore?"

Tayes propped her elbows on her knees and dropped her head, chuckling. "I'd piss myself from laughing if for one second I thought you were serious about hitting the streets and bringing down justice. You're too scared to leave The White Tower."

"So it's only a coincidence you told Weston about our setup? You pinned the ratings and the business on me."

"It's the truth," Tayes said. She was starting to think that Barbra had been right about the eldar juice. There was a bit more paranoia to Hobbes' attitude then normal. "And I don't see what the big deal is. That's how you and I have always run things."

"The ratings have been bad, and the board is looking to shake things up."

"So?"

"So." Hobbes tapped his desk as if pointing to unequivocal evidence. "You are gunning for my job."

"And you are a fool." Tayes stood. She had heard enough. She had a city to run and didn't have time to listen to a whiny baby whine about stupid cack. "I do what I do. Good luck finding anyone who does it better."

"Sit back down." Hobbes stood, as if his taller height would give him power. "I am your boss."

"You've never been my boss." Tayes turned her back to him. She did not have time to waste talking to a juiced up memory junkie. "You can threaten to write me up or to have me exported, but you won't 'cause you know that would piss me off. I know all the dirt. If I wanted to cause you damage, I could."

Hobbes' cheeks flushed, and he clenched his lips so tight they turned a soft white. "You will regret this."

"Try me." She stormed out of his office and gave him one final look over her shoulder. "I'm not worried about it."

CHAPTER THIRTEEN

The last time Randdol had felt so excited was during sex, but sex wasn't perfect. It brought nervousness, and he had to worry about things like his heart or stamina. The excitement he felt now was different. It came with a Zen-like peace.

Gently, as if holding a sacred relic, Randdol lifted the single cartridge of flame-grilled steak patty off its shelf.

Now was the time!

He set the cartridge into the MicroPot and waited. Before it was done, he could smell the charred meat, and he salivated at the thought of the juices oozing out of the patty.

The MicroPot dinged, and he carried the warm cartridge to his living area. Normally he ate in the kitchen standing up, but with such a special treat, he wanted to go all out. He'd laid a sheet on the floor and treated it as if he were having a picnic.

In his head, the wordcast streamed a much quieter piece than it usually did before the evening affirmation. The music was lush, with stringed instruments and a melody that kept rising and churning. It was arousing, and he fought to keep at bay the mental images of a nude Evelyn eating plump raspberries. It's not that he was opposed to such thoughts, more that tonight was supposed to be about the steak patty, and he didn't want Evelyn taking that away from him.

Packaged with the steak patty was a pile of mashed potatoes. They were creamy and glistened with butter. Bacon and chives scattered the potato peaks. For half a second, Randdol was tempted to try them first, but the patty called to him. He needed it.

The steak patty had an hourglass shape with deep diagonal seers running across its top. Along the charcoaled lines were crispy caramelized bits that oozed with juices.

Using the side edge of a fork, Randdol cut into the steak. It was so tender that the fork slid through it with ease. He stabbed the loose chunk of meat and placed it into his mouth.

The patty melted, running across his tongue.

Randdol's lips puckered, and he winced. A putrid bitter taste, like an old metallic coin dipped in sulfur for good measure, filled his mouth. He tried to spit out the steak patty, but it was so dissolved that he couldn't get rid of it. As his tongue hit the air, the chemical flavors intensified, and he heaved, unable to take a fresh breath.

Rushing to the kitchen, Randdol shoved his whole head under the faucet. He gargled and spit, but still the foul taste wouldn't leave his mouth.

As a last resort, he scrambled to the bathroom and pulled out a half-used bottle of rubbing alcohol. Taking a swig, he swished it around like mouthwash. The alcohol dried out his mouth and was far from pleasant, and yet the flavor and tingly sensation was better than the steak patty flavor.

Lines of drool swung from Randdol's chin, reaching to the bathroom counter. He wiped them away with the back of his hand, and then snorted, hacking out a wad of mucus.

It took a second swish of the rubbing alcohol and two full rinses of water before Randdol could think about anything other than the rancid taste in his mouth.

Regaining his composure, he hobbled back to his make-shift

picnic and inspected the steak patty food cartridge. His first thought was that the cartridge itself had been damaged, but he saw no punctures or dents. However, as he turned it over, he saw a tiny date stamped on the bottom in white. The steak patty cartridge was more than two years expired.

Randdol wanted to take the cartridge and throw it against the wall. He wanted to beat someone's skull in for it, and yet all he could do was throw back his head and laugh. Of course this would have happened. It was a fitting reminder of the horrible world he lived in and how soon everything would be different.

Feeling more invigorated by his plans, Randdol returned to the bathroom to set up. He lined the counter with a fresh towel and stacked two others beside it. On the clean towel, he laid out a pair of rusty pliers, a small steak knife, and a pile of shredded rags. The rags were stained with grease, blood, and unknown green marks, but he knew they were clean.

Tilting his neck from side to side, he cracked it. He did the same with his knuckles. There was a proper order he would have to do this. He decided the first thing had to be his hand device. Then he would do his teeth.

Randdol placed the tip of the knife against the webbing between his thumb and pointer finger. He traced the rim of the tag and settled on the top edge. With slow and steady pressure, he drove the knife into his flesh and made a single cut. Blood spilled forth, pooling in the folds of his wrinkles.

He used his right thumb and placed it below the tag. Pushing up, as if trying to remove a splinter, he squeezed his flesh. The blood oozing from his self-inflicted wound faded as blackness replaced it.

Squeezing harder, an amorphous blob spilled from the cut, embedded in it was the tag. It looked so much smaller than it had felt when embedded in his hand.

With the gel and tag out, blood once more dripped from the cut, so Randdol tied a rag sideways across his palm. It hurt, but he could endure. The incident with the raspberry thorns had been worse, and so would be what was coming next.

He clamped the pliers around his right back molar. The angle made it hard to grasp tight, and he had to stoop over, twisting his waist before he felt he had a solid grip. He gave the tooth a gentle tug as a test, and, confident he had it, he jerked it a second time, pulling with all his strength.

There was a flash of pain. Sharp pain. Pain like he'd never felt before and then blackness.

∼

Randdol's head hurt. His jaw throbbed and tingled. To his surprise, he lay on the floor of his bathroom, and it took a minute to piece together that he'd blacked out.

He still held the pliers, and on the floor beside them was his tooth. He could see now it wasn't a regular tooth. The x-rays he'd seen in his drugged-up state had been real. That was good. Part of him had been worried that the dentist operating had been a figment of his imagination, but now he knew the truth. They were real and something was inside his teeth.

The molar appeared to be ceramic, but instead of roots, it had a threaded base like a screw. By jerking it out with the pliers, he'd stripped the hole in his gums. That explained the blood he tasted, and why it was a lot less than what he expected.

Staggering, he used the counter and pulled himself back to his feet. Blood drenched his shirt, but he wasn't worried about it. What concerned him was a red, disc-shaped imprint on his forehead. He had fainted and then hit his head. There was no telling how long he'd been knocked out. That meant The Brigade could arrive any second. He had to move fast.

He secured the pliers on his back left molar, only this time instead of jerking the fake tooth free he spun it. The tooth twisted, and it only took four full rotations to unscrew it. The best part was that there was no new additional pain or blood.

In the mirror, he inspected his mouth. On the back right of his jaw was a gaping hole that still bled, while on the right was a tiny, threaded knob.

Randdol balled up the corner of a rag, placed it over his wound, and bit down to hold it in place. It would be awhile, but he suspected that it would stop bleeding.

Gathering his cane, Randdol stopped at the clock in the kitchen. It was 8:03p.m. The evening affirmation had started two minutes ago, and for the first time in his life, he hadn't heard it. That single thing made the pain in his jaw and hand worth it.

CHAPTER FOURTEEN

Randdol heard the sirens of the hoverlifts. He was already three blocks away from his apartment building, and if his plans had gone right, The Brigade had no way to track him.

That didn't stop him from walking faster though. He only had a few more streets to go, and then it would be impossible for brigadiers to find him.

After his inspired lunch with Banner, Randdol had made use of his work computer in an unauthorized manner. He told the scrubbers to search not the intranet, but the historical records to locate anything relating to the White Tower and The Word.

Most of what came back was useless, but the scrubbers had sniffed out the blueprints for The White Tower. The building was a fortress, but Randdol had pinpointed a single weakness.

To protect The Brigade and The Word from The Opposition, the tower received its water supply from deep underground. Built in the basement of the tower was a water filtration system, and if Randdol guessed right, he had a way to reach it. From there he could get into the White Tower. Once inside, he'd track down The Word and extract vengeance.

Randdol turned the corner of a blue-lit street and smiled at the sight of the connivance store. The place that had introduced him to Evelyn would be the same to help him get his revenge.

"You back, mister?" the chunky woman said. She now wore a feathered bra and boy briefs. Both were too tight for someone of her size. "Decided after all you want to party?"

Randdol tried to speak, but with the bloody rag still hanging from his mouth, the words came out garbled.

"I don't want any trouble." The clerk looked from the tail of the rag to the blood on Randdol's shirt. "Do what you want with me, but don't take my credit hours."

Randdol pulled the wadded rag out of his mouth. He could still taste blood, but the wound had congealed and no longer gushed. "I'm not here for you."

Knowing the woman would use her tag to call The Brigade, Randdol wasted no time. He hooked the handle of his cane onto the nearest bookshelf and tugged. It topped over, the wood breaking as adult toys spilled all over of the floor.

The metal sheet was still wedged into the hole in the wall, so that at first glance it looked like nothing more than a metal frame for the building.

Randdol kicked out the sheet. It flipped backwards, sliding down the stairs.

"What is cucking going on?" The woman seemed to have overcome her fear and now stood shoulder to shoulder with Randdol, both looking into the hole. "Did you know that was there?"

Randdol ignored her. She was nothing—a fly not worth swatting.

Climbing through the hole, Randdol made his way to the grow room. The lights still burned bright, and the raspberries smelled like heaven. Evelyn slinked into his thoughts, and he banished her. Later, he would have time to think of her.

Using his cane again, Randdol jimmied the tip into the grate that had tripped him. He pushed down and pried it open, its rusted metal scraping against the brick floor. As it moved, it shredded the vines and popped berries, leaving a trail of juice.

"Do you think they are edible?" The woman's eyes were wide, and she leaned in to sniff a white raspberry blossom.

"You only have minutes before The Brigade arrives." Randdol knew The Brigade would need someone to blame when they couldn't find him. They would pin the hole in the wall, him missing, and the raspberries on the clerk. Randdol didn't feel guilty. If she had been smart and called in The Brigade the second he knocked over the bookshelf, they might have let her slide. Now she was done for and might as well enjoy the time she had left. "If you're going for the raspberries, don't waste your time."

"Raspberries." The woman repeated the word in a stilted manner as if she were saying it for the first time.

Randdol jumped into the hole that the metal grate had covered. He braced himself, expecting a long fall, but the channel beneath the room was only four feet deep. Feeling it out with his foot and cane, he determined it ran at a slight slant and was concrete, not brick.

Ducking his head, he could still stand, and he plodded forward, into the darkness. From behind, he could hear the sloppy sounds of the clerk eating berries.

The darkness engulfed Randdol.

He had been a fool for not thinking about bringing matches or a torch of some kind. To his relief, the crawl space he traveled down curved right and opened into a large funnel that had hanging lamps from the ceiling. The lights were a yellow, but a fuzzy mold grew on them, casting an emerald light across what must have been an old sewer.

The tunnel branched in three directions. Along the outer edges was a raised platform with railings, while the middle sunk, as if for holding water. Mighty arches, twenty feet high, bridged the ceiling.

Randdol had two concerns. First, he had to get farther away from the connivance store so The Brigade wouldn't find him. Then he had to navigate his way to the water filtration system. It dawned on him that maybe his plan to break into The White Tower hadn't been so clean-cut as he thought. It hadn't occurred to him to search for blueprints or a map to lead him through Hata's underside.

Deciding that any direction was as good as another, he turned right, following the tunnel. Past the intersection, he noticed alcoves in the walls, every fifty feet or so, and after the fourth one, he stopped to inspect it.

The alcove appeared to be a human-sized notch cut into the wall, but when he jammed his cane into the shadows, it struck something hard. Dropping to his knees, he felt around with his hands and discovered a hatch with a plaque embedded in it. He fingered the words and determined that it read, "Hata Service Hatch 34." Below it read, "Alexander Industries."

Randdol had no idea where a service hatch would lead but guessed it was somewhere more useful than a sewer. He spun the lever on the hatch, and the round porthole opened. Inside he only saw darkness, but in feeling around he located the rungs of a ladder.

The Brigade would come soon. Better to face darkness than them. Holding his cane outstretched over the hatch, he let it go. The cane clanged, and after fifteen seconds the noise stopped. The hatch was deep, but wasn't too far for him to climb. All those many days walking up and down the stairs to his ninth-floor apartment were finally going to pay off.

Sliding into the hatch, he closed the porthole behind him. Now he was confident The Brigade would have no way of locating him. He only hoped he could find his way out of wherever service hatch thirty-four ended. Using his cane, he pulled it shut above him, covering himself in full darkness.

CHAPTER FIFTEEN

The moment Tayes entered the connivance store and saw the hole in the wall, she regretted not having sent brigaders to inspect the shop after Randdol's first disappearance. This was on her. If she didn't fix it, Hobbes would finally have a real reason to kick her out of Hata.

Back at Randdol's apartment, brigaders had found the old man's tags and the pulled teeth. Somehow, he'd figured out their system for tracking citizens and now was off the grid.

Stepping over an arm-sized dildo, Tayes peered into the hole. The blue light on the other side had a mystical quality to it. On the vid screen in her helmet, she pulled up the blueprints for the block. Below the connivance store was a channel that connected to the city's runoff water system. The undercity was a labyrinth. She would never be able to track Randdol down there, but that was okay, because her gut told her Randdol's final destination, even if he didn't realize it. He was going to Old Hata.

The last time Tayes had been in Old Hata was the day The Word and The Brigade came. That was twenty-seven years ago, and the memories of that night haunted her.

Tayes couldn't remember what she and her parents had done earlier that night. They must have eaten dinner. From what she could recall, her mom was a horrible cook, which meant her father had prepared it.

It had been around bedtime when she'd gone to the kitchen to kiss her parents goodnight. The kitchen was old style, with a real wood table and stone tiles. The walls were painted bright colors—none of the white bland cack that plastered Hata today.

Tayes knew what guns were, but at that age, she'd never seen one in real life. She was filled with shock to find her father holding a gun against her mother. His wrist shook, as if the gun were heavy, and a mixture of sweat and tears ran down his red cheeks.

"You don't have to do this," her mother said. "You don't have to listen to him."

"I do." Her father brought the butt of the gun up, tapping it against his temple. "The Word says I have to. The Word never lies."

"What of Catherine?" her mother said. "Your flesh and blood. You can't do this to her. It will kill her."

"Mom?" Catherine asked in a quiet voice. "What is going on?"

"I'm serving the will of The Word." Her father knelt, keeping the gun pointed at her mother. With his free hand, he waved to Catherine, gesturing her over.

Catherine looked to her mother. The woman's thin nightgown clung to her. Tear stains dotted her chest, and when she met Catherine's eyes, she shook her head, telling Catherine not to listen.

Catherine knew the consequences of not listening to The Word. No matter how desperate her father might try not to hurt her or her mother, he wouldn't have the will power to disobey.

"Please, Papa." Catherine crossed the kitchen, staying just out her father's reach. "Put the gun away. I'm scared."

"You don't know The Word," he said. "Anyone who doesn't know The Word is The Opposition."

Catherine hated The Word. He always made her parents and the other adults do strange things. She dreaded the day when she would be old enough to have The Word's thought box installed. Luckily, that was years away and wouldn't happen till she turned seventeen. For now, at least, she was free.

"Don't do this," her mother pleaded again.

"I am the will of The Word." Her father pulled the trigger of the gun.

Catherine heard a popping sound. There was a flash of light, and when it faded, she saw that her father had a butcher's knife protruding from his chest.

"Run, Catherine," her mother yelled. "Run and never stop running."

Her father pulled the trigger of the gun again. Her mother fell.

Catherine didn't look back. She turned her head and sprinted. In seconds she was out the screen door of their kitchen and on the streets of Hata. The air was sticky and the pavement warm against her bare feet.

Others fled their homes, and the streets filled with those that did not serve The Word. Gunfire, which might be heard as a distant pop, now rattled the windows of the buildings. Children smudged with dirt and blood sat, crying, on the curbs. Parents shrieked in anger. The sky itself was ablaze as two of the tallest skyscrapers downtown burned. The city was falling.

A group of six brigaders blocked the end of the street in front of Catherine. They wore black armor and scary helmets that made them look like space bugs. Catherine knew who they were. All children knew of them. Brigaders were the ones that came at night and took kids who were bad, though sometimes they took the parents too. It seemed to Catherine that The Brigade took whomever they wanted.

The brigaders raised their guns, and with no verbal warning, they opened fire into the streets.

Catherine dropped flat onto her belly. Bullets pierced the air above her and ripped into those still foolish enough to be standing.

Death screams filled the night, and blood rained down on Catherine, drizzling her in a red mist.

The gunfire lasted only a minute, but it felt like hours. When it stopped, Catherine raised her head to see if any others still lived. No one moved except her and the brigaders.

The words Catherine's mother spoke played again in her head. "Run and never stop running." As much as Catherine wanted to listen, she knew running was a death sentence. There was no escape.

One by one, the brigaders checked those lying on the ground. When one of them got to Catherine, she rolled between their feet, slipping behind them. She grabbed the brigader's wrist and turned his own gun on him.

It was the first-time Catherine had killed, and it wouldn't be the last. She had no regrets.

"I'll kill you all!" Catherine fired again. The kick was too much, and it tumbled from her hands.

The remaining brigaders aimed their guns at Catherine.

"Hold your fire," a man said. He was a white man and the only one not in armor. He wore a suit and tie, and an old-style newspaper hat.

Making a fist, Catherine ran as hard as she could and plowed into the man, driving her tiny knuckles into his side. The two of them toppled over, and she unleashed a furry of scratches, aimed at his face.

A fist thudded into the back of Catherine's head, and three pairs of hands jerked her off the man.

"I'm perfectly fine." The man rose to his feet, dusting off his suit. "I could have handled a mere child."

"What do you want us to do with her, sir?" a brigader asked.

The man's mouth formed an evil smile. "Send her to the academy."

"But sir, she's br—"

"Am I not The Word?" the man said. "Do I need to speak?"

The Word, the father of The Brigade, and the one responsible for her parent's death, now stood in front of Catherine. She had been so close to hurting him, maybe even killing him.

Kneeling so he was eye level with her, The Word reached out and ran a hand along her cheek. "I should have you killed, but there is a fire in you. A fire that can't be taught, and so instead of wasting that fire, I will make sure you burn who I want you to burn."

That was the first time Tayes had met The Word and the last time she had seen Old Hata. Visiting the forgotten city terrified her, but she had no choice. There was no one else she could trust to hunt down Randdol Mupt.

CHAPTER SIXTEEN

Randdol knew he'd reached the bottom of the shaft when he lifted a foot and instead of his heel catching on a new rung, it stomped on solid ground. Feeling around, he located his cane. Tracing its sides, he couldn't find a single dent in it. It had survived its fall.

Opposite the ladder was a metal door with a crank wheel. As he spun the lever, the door creaked open, and a crack of light trickled into the shaft.

On the other side of the door was a sprawling city. It looked like Hata, which made zero sense. He had climbed downward for almost thirty minutes. He couldn't have climbed down and then end back up at street level, could he? No, it had to be something else, something older.

The shaft that Randdol descended was built into a metal wall that rose twenty stories before passing the reach of the streetlights that shined below. Toward where he thought The White Tower should stand, he saw what must have once been skyscrapers. Now they were broken, sprouting out of rubble piles made of concrete and broken steel.

From what he could tell, this city had a near identical layout to Hata. That was amazing news, because it meant it shouldn't be too hard for Randdol to figure out the location under The White Tower, and from there figure a way to get back to the surface.

Heading west, the street before him lay in wreckage; the asphalt cracked and the nearest building was reduced to a broken pile of bricks. The storefronts looked greasy and scorch marks splattered the few places where walls still stood.

The streetlights were spaced at odd intervals with deep shadows between them, reminding Randdol of his childhood. Something about this city felt familiar. A thought occurred to him. Was this Hata? The real Hata? The place where he had spent his younger years? It made no sense, and yet somehow it made perfect sense.

He racked his brain, trying to remember, but not once could he think of a new city being built or remember moving from this Hata to the above Hata he lived in.

The heel of his cane struck something. The object rolled out of the shadows and into the dim streetlight. It settled and looked back at him with two hollow eye sockets. It was a skull, and from what he could feel with his feet, there were plenty more on the ground.

Whatever this version of Hata had been, something awful had happened here. Something so awful that everyone abandoned the city and built a new one on the remains. Was this the work of The Opposition?

If so, why couldn't he remember? What had happened to his own memories that he could remember this place, but not what happened here or leaving it?

Ahead of Randdol, the next three city blocks were in utter ruins. Buildings that had stood several stories high were nothing but piles. There was no way he could climb the mounds. He had to go around.

The deeper he got into the city, the more he thought about turning back all together. The worst was when he found a scattered pile of bones and saw that the skulls were noticeably smaller than the ones he'd previously seen. Some even had bullet holes going right through them.

The Brigade, as horrible as they were, would arrest him and send him to a labor city. He would surely die there, but he might live longer there than he would here.

A shadow moved across the street ahead of him.

Randdol froze and slowed his breathing, unsure if it was a trick of the light or if something had actually moved.

A rapid tapping sound, like hard rain on a window, rose from the shadows, and as it did, a hulking mass shifted between two buildings. The thing, whatever it was, had to be two or three stories high, and unlike Randdol it seemed to be unfazed by the darkness.

The most unsettling thing about the mass was the way it moved. It didn't walk so much as slunk across the street, waddling from one alley to another. The thing smelled like the rotten steak patty had tasted. Like death.

Sweat formed on Randdol's brow, and he did everything he could to keep still. After three minutes, the pattering rain faded and the hulking creature was gone, lost in the shadows.

Not wanting to meet whatever it was, Randdol moved in the opposite direction, towards the center of the city. Going through the downtown area would put him out of the way, but he'd rather walk an extra mile than face whatever monster had been hiding in the shadows.

CHAPTER SEVENTEEN

Past the heart of downtown, Randdol found a rare sight—a solid wall with a ten-foot piece of graffiti on it. It was the eye-cog symbol The Word used for propaganda. The same one that Banner had showed him at work. The only difference was underneath the creepy eye. Instead of the words "Resist them," it read, "Resist The Word."

Randdol scratched his head, dumbfounded. For the symbol to be used down here and in that manner, it meant that this city must have been part of The Opposition. That suggested it was The Brigade that had destroyed it, and somewhere along the line The Word had stolen their propaganda and used it against them.

As his mind toyed with which of his memories might not be real, he became aware of the quiet. The quiet inside his head was too quiet, to the point of distraction. Without the music of the wordcast, he felt alone and cut off from the rest of the world.

At this time of night, the wordcast would play a simple piano piece. Something soothing that would make one feel calmed and at peace. Randdol wished he could hear it, and he wondered if he would be able to fall asleep without it playing.

He couldn't remember a time when his thoughts felt so loud. In a way, he needed the wordcast because without it his thoughts were yelling at him.

Reaching a darker section of the street, Randdol paused and shifted his weight off his cane. For a good two hundred yards all the streetlights before him were out. He toyed with the idea of going around the shadowy area, but his final destination, the equivalent of where The White Tower should stand, was on the other side. The fastest way out of this apocalyptic city was straight though.

The darkness was so overwhelming that Randdol couldn't see his feet and resorted to sweeping his cane along the ground before every step. The shaft of the cane knocked a chunk of something that sounded like concrete. It shook, and crumbs of the concrete spilled onto the sidewalk. In the distance, the same hard rain he'd heard earlier rose up, as if responding to the noise that Randdol had made.

Increasing his pace, Randdol came to an intersection. Half a block to his left he could see the silhouette of something human. The thing walked down the street, heading right for him.

The human shape carried no lights, and Randdol hoped that whatever the thing was, it too couldn't see in the dark. Sinking to the ground, Randdol lay as flat as he could, trying to hide himself behind a chunk of concrete with rebar jutting at bent angles. If he stayed quiet, there was a good chance the thing would bypass him without realizing.

The shuffling of feet grew louder. Boots hit rubble and stones slid. It was like the sound of an old-style clock, and with each tick-tock, it came closer.

Bright lights blinded Randdol.

"Randdol Mupt," the thing said. "You are under arrest."

Peering through the cracks of his fingers, Randdol realized his mistake. The human thing had been a brigader with their external helmet lights turned off. It must have shut down the lights to use their infrared tracker.

"I'm not going back," Randdol said. "If you are going to kill me, you need to do it now."

The sound of rain once more pummeled Randdol's ears.

The Brigader turned, redirecting their helmet light down the street. They were weak, but stretched far enough to show that the hulking creature had returned.

From their equipment belt, the brigader pulled a cylindrical tube. Shaking the device, it popped the top off. It made a clicking sound, like the seal of a bottle being broken, and then a beam of sparkling fire formed on the other end.

The brigader threw the flare. It spun in the air and landed inches from the monster's feet. A red searing light washed over the creature. Its flesh was a dark grey, almost black, with patches of mold and fungus growing across its hide. It had huge ears, like sails, and two tusks jutted from the sides of its mouth—both stained dark, and one broken. Its eyes were red.

The monstrous thing shook like a dog. Pellets of concrete and rubble flung from its back, crashing into the surrounding buildings.

"Well, cack," the brigader said. "That kind of day, I guess."

CHAPTER EIGHTEEN

An elongated skin flap that sprouted from where the monster's nose should have been inflated. The air rushed out the other end, making a trumpeting sound.

The thing rose on two legs and then brought its front legs down hard, stomping out the flare. Darkness once more flooded the street.

"Run," the brigader commanded.

Adrenaline kicked in, and Randdol wanted to run. His aches and pains meant nothing, but even with his cane, the street was too cluttered with broken concrete. A single misstep could mean impaling himself on rebar.

"Get your ass going!" The brigader hooked an elbow under Randdol's armpit and jerked him forward. "We only have to make it to the bridge. It won't cross the water."

"I can't see where I'm going." Randdol tried to explain why he kept losing his balance.

"I should let you die here."

Randdol thought the brigader was going to throw him to the

ground, but instead the brigader slowed enough for Randdol to match their pace.

"What is that thing?" Randdol asked.

"Leftover from the war."

The brigader practically dragged Randdol. He was doing his best to keep his feet moving. More just lifting and pushing off the ground to keep his weight up while relying on the brigader to keep him moving in the right direction.

They passed through the darkest shadows of the street. The lamps on the other side now backlit the cluttered road so that Randdol could just make out where he was placing his feet.

"I can see now." Randdol jerked his arm, intending to pull free of the brigader, but the brigader held tight.

"I'm not taking any chance," the brigader said. "Not this close to the bridge."

The ground shook as the beast closed the distance between it and its prey. Its form hunkered after them, gliding over the bones of fallen buildings as if it were doing nothing more than walking through shallow water.

"Two more blocks," the brigader said.

"We won't make it!"

"Cack licks." The brigader skidded to a halt. "I'm going to take heat for this."

The brigader let go of Randdol and pulled a fist-size orb off their belt. The brigader twisted its top and then pressed down the center. The sphere sparkled with light.

The brigader cocked an arm and threw the orb. It bounced twice before exploding. A dark, grassy-colored gas rose into the air, spreading across the street like a sentient mist.

The lights on the orb sparkled again, and this time when they did, the mist caught fire, forming a literal wall of flames between them and the beast.

"That won't stop it," the brigader said. "Keep running for the bridge."

Randdol did as told, though he was back to moving at more of a fast walk than a run.

A blaring shriek rose from behind the fire wall. Then the shadow of the creature appeared, plowing through the flames. The monster tripped. Its lesion-covered body rolled, crashing into a four-story apartment building. The structure collapsed, but instead of stopping the monster, it only seemed to enrage it more. The thing let out a defiant trumpet and charged the brigader.

"Cack cack cackity cack!" The brigader ran, following Randdol.

Randdol had already reached the bridge and was making his way across. It was wide enough only for foot traffic, and its railings had a floral flourish design of intertwining vines and leaves.

The bridge spanned a fifty-foot chasm. The walls of both sides were metal and dropped straight down. From below, Randdol could hear the sound of rushing water, but it was too far into the darkness for him to see it.

Reaching the bridge, the brigader drew their gun and fired three rounds at the beast. One spike missed, but the other two burrowed into the creature's face. Arcs of electricity shot between the two spikes. The monster didn't even seem to notice.

"Well, cack." The brigader sheathed the gun and followed Randdol onto the bridge. "Haul your ass! This truck is coming and it ain't stopping for nothing!"

Reaching the other side of the bridge, Randdol dropped to his hands and knees. His heart pounded as he labored for every breath. It felt like something heavy was sitting on his chest, and he couldn't get enough air.

A crunching sound drew his attention. The brigader was a quarter of the way across the pedestrian bridge when the monster charged on. Its feet were wider than the bridge, and whatever supports kept it suspended weren't enough to hold the creature's massive weight.

The bridge shook and buckled.

The monster let out a final trumpeting sound as the bridge collapsed around it, dumping the creature down into the dark chasm.

A thunderous cracking sound ripped through the air as the last of the supports gave way. The bridge fell, but not all at once. It melted like a stick of butter slowly being warmed. The furthest end sank, and with every second it dropped lower and lower, which meant that as the brigader ran, the slope of the bridge became steeper and steeper till the point where the whole thing swung out of Randdol's sight.

Crawling to the edge of the chasm, Randdol looked down to see that the remains of the bridge lay flat, like a rope ladder. The brigader, using the railings, was scrambling up the side.

Randdol waited and watched.

The clock ticked by, and by some miracle the brigader reached the top of bridge, but due to a twisted railing, the brigader couldn't pull themselves up and around the edge of the chasm.

"I need a hand," the brigader said.

Randdol lay prone, on his stomach, but before extending his cane to the brigader, he stopped. If he saved the brigader, that guaranteed his arrest and being taken in. Is that what he wanted?

"You're going to let me fall, aren't you?" Panic sounded in the brigader's voice.

Randdol hooked his cane handle into the finger grip of the brigader's gun and pulled it in.

"What are you doing?" the brigader asked.

"I'm going to need that when I get into The White Tower."

"You can't let me fall."

"What does The Brigade like to say?" Randdol palmed the gun. It felt like power. "Beware The Opposition..."

"Don't." The soldier said it halfheartedly, as if they knew it didn't matter.

Randdol swung his cane, cracking the metal handle against the brigader's helmet. Glass shattered into the brigader's face.

Losing their grip, the brigader screamed and fell into the chasm.

Randdol counted to ten, but heard no splash. He decided the fall must be so far, or the brigader's body so small, it was impossible to hear it from all the way up here.

With his cane gone, walking was problematic, but in exchange he now had a gun, and that was far more important. He had big plans for the gun. It was what he was going to use to kill The Word.

CHAPTER NINETEEN

In the darkness, Tayes slammed against something hard. The air rushed out of her chest, and she fumbled for anything to hold onto. Whatever she'd hit must have been sloped because before she could recover from the fall, she skidded deeper into the chasm.

The sound of running water grew closer as she went over another ledge. Doing her best to upright herself, she crossed her legs and kept her boots pointed down. She gripped her arms around her chest and held her body stiff. If the fall was too high, her legs would snap, and she'd drown. If the water was too shallow, she could break every bone in her body.

She hit the water and went under.

Instinct and years of training kicked in. She threw her body into an L-shape, which redirected her momentum and curved her back to the surface.

Tayes had learned the maneuver during her early days at the academy. Dozens of times, she had jumped, or been thrown from a hoverlift, into the bay surrounding Hata. She had never thought the technique would ever be needed, but now she was grateful she knew it.

She cleared the water away from her eyes, mouth, and nose before taking a single sip of the air. Old Hata was a contaminated wasteland, and there was no telling what bacteria or worse things could be in the water. In the best-case scenario, a single drop of the wrong stuff could lead to a week of diarrhea, while in the worst-case situation, she could end up dead.

The one benefit to being trapped in a chasm filled with water, hundreds of feet down, was that it had to flow somewhere, and she knew where. This whole channel fed the water filtration system. All she had to do was tread water and enjoy the ride.

Ditching her broken helmet, Tayes swam to the chasm wall and used it as a guide to determine which way the water flowed. Once she knew, she paddled along with it, at a light pace.

After ten minutes the channel curved, and she heard splashing, like a boat propeller. Above the waterline was a stacked series of lights, and she could make out a ladder running upwards to a catwalk. Tayes hooked an elbow onto the ladder's side and snagged her knee around one of the bars. The current tried to push her, but she had just enough leverage to lift herself out of the water. Standing on a dry rung, she took a moment to survey her surroundings.

What she thought sounded like a motor or propeller was the hulking monster. The beast had been sucked flush against a vertical metal grate. Too big to fit between the bars, and not strong enough to move against the current, it was pinned in place.

Tayes had seen the monster once before, almost fifteen years ago. The thing had broken out of Old Hata and gotten into the undercity. Squads of brigaders tried to stop it, but their weapons were useless against the beast. It was Tayes who, instead of focusing on killing the creature, formed a plan to lead it back to the fallen city.

Rumors swirled throughout The Brigade, and no one knew exactly what the monster was. Some said it was an advance war machine, others claimed it was a mutated creature changed through chemical attacks, and some claimed it was a supernatural being.

In the dim light, Tayes couldn't make out the details of the creature. Whatever it was, it had the ability to swim or float. She expected it would continue to do so until it no longer could. If it were a robot, it might spend years or centuries stuck against the grate. If it were living, it might have days at most.

Shaking her head, Tayes clambered up the ladder and onto the catwalk. There a second ladder appeared to extend to the top of the chasm. It didn't interest her. She was done with Old Hata.

She followed the catwalk till its end. There she found an old-school mechanical door. A wheel jutted from the door's center. Throwing all her weight against the wheel, it creaked a few inches. She repeated the process and by the third try, it loosened so she could spin it with one hand.

Once on the other side, she made sure to seal the door. If memory served her, she was in the lower levels of the water filtration system. All around her were pipes and humming pumps. They went up, down, and burrowed into walls.

The plant was a maze, and she took far too long to find the central lift that would take her up into The White Tower. When she saw the lift controls, she grew concerned. A brigade member should have been watching them.

Tayes summoned the lift, and when it appeared, there was a limp brigader laying on it. She rolled the body over and retracted the helmet. It was the boy from the cafeteria, the one with the raviolis. He had no pulse, and his body was already growing cold.

Inspecting him, she found a bullet spike, jutting from just under his left armpit. There was no doubt in her mind: Randdol had shot the kid using her gun on its maximum setting.

If Tayes hadn't put him on duty here, he would still be alive and maybe a more experienced brigader could have stopped Randdol. Not only was she directly responsible for the boy's death, but her own gun had been used to kill him.

The logical side of her brain told her it wasn't her fault. Things happen in a place like Hata. Brigaders knew what kind of work they were getting into. Yet the warm side of her brain still hurt, and she regretted not knowing the boy's name.

Tayes unhooked the boy's gun from his belt and strapped it to her own. Randdol Mupt was dangerous, and she was going to stop him.

CHAPTER TWENTY

The second member of The Brigade that Randdol killed was on the lift as the two rode into The White Tower. The brigader had moved to draw their gun, and Randdol had killed them.

Randdol was still trying to decide if he was going to kill a third brigader. For now, he needed the third. The White Tower was far more of a labyrinth than he had realized, and the third brigader was his ticket to finding The Word.

"This won't end well for you," the brigader said. "What do you want me—"

Randdol pressed the barrel of the gun harder into The Brigade member's neck. "What I want is The Word. Take me to him or die. It's that simple."

The brigader looked down at the floor and continued walking down the white-walled hall.

With so many floors it was hard to keep track, but Randdol thought they were on the fifty-eighth level. He'd taken the service lift from the water treatment plant into The White Tower. From there he took the stairs to the third floor and acquired his current tour guide. The two of them had then backtracked to the second floor, found a tech lift, and taken it to an unmarked level where they walked up two flights of stairs.

"What you want is through those doors." The brigader pointed through a set of wide-swinging double doors.

"Show me." Randdol stepped aside to let The Brigade member take the lead.

The brigader waved his hand in front of the door's control panel. It registered his tag and swung open.

The room was a server farm.

Randdol felt a rush of cool air as the hum of electronics buzzed in his ears. Rows upon rows of steel towers lined the room, each filled with stacks of hard drives. Staggered strips of white lights ran down each row and offered the only illumination in the room. The high ceiling was drenched in shadows, and Randdol couldn't tell how far up it went.

"I don't understand," Randdol said. "Where is The Word?"

"This is The Word." The brigader waved around the room. "This is where all the wordcasts are streamed from. It can be accessed manually, but it's all run on an automated system."

"You're trying to trick me. This is some scam, and you've already leaked our location to the rest of The Brigade!"

"The console control system is near the center of the room." The brigader held his arms up, trying to make it clear they were not a threat. "I don't know how to use that cack, but I swear it's legit."

Randdol gestured with the gun barrel, motioning for the brigader to walk deeper into the room. The server farm was set up in a circular pattern with the towers all radiating out from the middle of the room. It reminded Randdol slightly of the eye with cogs he'd seen in the city below Hata.

At the room's center, the floor raised and a high-walled, square desk perched on it. A single set of stairs led up the platform.

"Show me how the computer works," Randdol said.

"I don't know how. I'm security, not a tech."

Randdol believed The Brigade member, so he pulled the trigger. A bullet spike, shot into the brigader's neck, hit right below his jawbone. Like a piece of trash, the brigader fell, twitching, to the floor.

Hobbling to the computer, Randdol wished he had his cane, but he had no regrets about the trade. The gun had served him well.

He waved his left hand over the console desk.

Nothing happened.

Randdol's cheeks flushed. He wasn't thinking. Of course the computer wouldn't recognize him. He no longer had a tag.

Grumbling, he limped back down the stairs to the dead brigader. Rummaging through The Brigade member's gear, he found a few grenades, but no knife.

With nothing else to use, Randdol kneeled. He lifted The Brigade member's left hand, holding it like a messy sandwich, and bit down. His teeth tore through the brigader's flesh. For reasons that Randdol didn't want to know, the man's hand tasted salty.

Through the fresh hole in the brigader's hand, Randdol squeezed out the man's tag. The gelatinous black goo pooled in Randdol's palm with the circular chip floating in the center.

Hiking back to the computer console, Randdol waved the tag and activated it. Vid screens hovered into place on all four sides of the station. Some showed gauges for pressure and temperature. Others had graphs mapping CPU usage. All of it was overwhelming and nothing like the computer at his work.

Taking a seat in a swiveling chair, Randdol spun, trying to make sense of all the screens. He stopped when he found a gridded spreadsheet that looked like a broadcast schedule. Each day of the week had blocks of times mapped out, and every day at 8:01 in the morning and evening the same file was set to play.

Randdol previewed one of the files and through the computer's speakers came a familiar voice.

"Resist them. Trust The Word. The Word will not lie. It is loyal to you. It wants you great. It wants you safe from The Opposition.

The Opposition wants to take. They want your freedom. They want your thoughts. They want you. The Opposition will come. When it does, resist them."

Randdol leaned back in his chair. The Brigade member hadn't been lying. The Word was not real. This computer was The Word.

CHAPTER TWENTY-ONE

Cuck. Horse. Cack. Burger. Meatus. The string of curses played so loud in Randdol's head it was as if The Word spoke them.

If The Word was a lie, and this computer proved it, what else was The Brigade lying about? Where was Evelyn? Was there even such a thing as labor cities, or was she dead and her body cast in a furnace somewhere? Randdol needed answers, and more importantly, he had to do something, but now he didn't know what.

"Resist them. Trust The Word. The Word will not lie. It is loyal to you. It wants you great. It wants you safe from The Opposition. The Opposition wants to take. They want your freedom. They want your thoughts. They want you. The Opposition will come. When it does, resist them."

The preview of the audio file looped a third time, but Randdol shut it off. In doing so, an idea struck him. After years of listening to The Word that was exactly what Randdol would do. The Word instructed him to "resist them," so he would, only "them" wasn't The Opposition. Them was The Word. Randdol would use The Word against itself. He would use the very system of control to set the citizens of Hata free.

The first thing Randdol did was access the room's control system. That was easy to do because it was a standard feature all HVAC systems had. Knowing other brigaders would soon be on his tail, he needed to put The White Tower, or at least the sever farm, into some sort of lock-down mode.

He played around with the time settings. It did nothing, but he got lucky when he upped the temperature control. A fire warning popped onto the vid screen. He manually overrode it and flagged the room as having a fire.

The doors to the sever farm slammed shut and huge whirling fans from somewhere above kicked in, blasting a torrent of rushing air down onto the severs. It was cold as hell, but it should do the job of keeping anyone else out.

Now, with extra time, he spun to face the main access for The Word. From what he could tell by the schedule, it seemed like all the audio files had an index number.

Randdol called up a scrubber search form and told the algorithm to find the full index of audio files. It did as commanded and reported back that there was a grand total of 549,092 files.

That was more files than he thought there would be. He'd hoped he could manipulate some of the files, and force The Word to say whatever Randdol wanted it to say, but that seemed out of the question.

While scrolling through the list, he noticed there was an import section. He accessed the import queue and was given the option of importing a historical file or live streaming a vid.

That was interesting. Maybe Randdol didn't need The Word. Maybe Randdol could speak to the citizens. Hearing someone else's voice in their heads would be a shock. It might be so jarring they would actually listen to whatever Randdol said.

Randdol began a new recording.

He opened his mouth to say something, but nothing came out.

He didn't know what to say.

He knew first hand that The Word was not real. He saw the computer that held the audio files. He saw the schedule. He could see how they looped around and would replay a message from ten years ago that no one would remember. How could he explain that so people could understand?

"Don't touch the computer again," a voice said from behind him.

Randdol spun in his rolling chair. Hidden in shadows was a female brigader. He could only see her from the waist down. Her armor was drenched in a strange brown sludge.

"I know the truth." Randdol grinned. The brigader didn't know the computer system was importing a live feed. He could use that to his advantage. "I know The Word isn't real."

The brigader laughed. "That's a good one. I've had a rough day, but the worst was when you bashed in my helmet."

"That was you?" Randdol asked.

"Yes, and here I am, still fighting." She stepped from the shadows. She was pretty, with a slightly upturned nose and dark, almost red hair. Her skin was an exotic chestnut color.

"You're black."

"Brown," she said. "I know it's been awhile since you've seen a non-white person, so I don't expect you to know the difference, but there is a difference. I'm brown."

"No." Randdol spoke with authority as if his words had the power to change reality. This had to be another trick. It made no sense. "You are messing with my head. You are a lie, just like The Word is a lie."

She laughed again, but this time harder and more girly as if she was embracing her female traits just to piss him off. "I had to crawl through a sewage pipe to get in here, and I wasn't sure if it would be worth it, but now... now I'm sure."

"What are you talking about?"

"I've watched the footage, but this is the first time I've been a part of one of the reveals." Stepping out of the shadows, she stood only a few feet from the stairs leading to the console. "I never knew how satisfying it would feel to do this."

"To do what?"

"To tell you, Randdol, that you are The Word."

CHAPTER TWENTY-TWO

Joy surged through Tayes' body. She'd never known that doing something so simple as telling the truth could be so rewarding, and the best part was she hadn't even told all the truth yet. Not even the worst of it.

"You-are-lying!" Randdol yelled so loud that his voice cracked. "The Word is nothing but a computer system. I've seen the files!"

"You recorded those decades ago and a full library of phonetic sounds."

"I'd know if I were The Word," he said. "And I'd recognize my own voice."

"When we hear our voices, they sound different than when we hear recordings of them. Plus, you are a bit older and your memories have been messed with."

"That isn't a thing."

"It's true," she said. "Your memories are still there. We can't remove or overwrite them, but we did put them behind a wall."

"Stop. Just stop!"

What made a person a person was something Tayes didn't have

the answer to. Memories were important, and yet even with his memories scrubbed, Randdol was still very Randdol. She could see it written onto his face: the disdain directed at her, the shock of seeing a woman in power.

The Randdol Mupt that Tayes knew was showing his true self. The bottled-up rage that would lash out at whatever was near. She could end this now, a quick shot from her gun would drop him, but she didn't want this to come to a rapid end. She wanted to drag out his pain as long as possible.

"Tell me about your wife or daughter," she said.

"I don't have a wife or daughter."

"Sure you do."

Randdol held the sides of his head. "You're lying."

To Tayes' knowledge, this was the first time that someone had ever told Randdol the truth. Every other time he had discovered it for himself. Telling him was like trying to convince someone who had never seen the color cobalt what the color looked like. How do you point out the things they cannot see? "Tell me anything about your life prior to the time you turned forty."

"I'm not answering," he said.

Tayes raised her gun ever so slightly, reminding him of who was in control.

"I..." He grimaced, as if thinking. His gaze looked passed her. His eyes jittered back and forth. "It was... it was a long time ago."

"What did the house look like where you grew up?"

"That was a long time ago."

"Describe anywhere you've lived before. Anywhere prior to the place you live now."

"I don't know," Randdol said in a raised voice.

"I remember where I grew up," Tayes said. "It was a Victorian house in the suburbs. It didn't have central heat or air. It was at one point painted white, but the paint had cracked, leaving aged wooden shingles behind. We lived there till I was eight. After that we moved to Old Hata. That's when The Word came. That's when you came."

"More lies."

"You ordered my father to kill me." Tayes couldn't help but remember the smell of sweat as she watched the tears roll down her father's face. "I escaped him only to be captured by brigaders."

"You are bla—brown," Randdol said. "Brigaders would have killed you."

"I'm sure they would have, but I pissed off the right person and I was sent to the academy. At first I thought it was because The Brigade found sick pleasure in perverting me to hunt and chase down my people, but later I learned I was there for your perverted pleasure."

She smiled in the way she did when her cat chased its own tail and then accidentally clawed itself. Randdol had no clue, and he wasn't even close to figuring it out yet, but as much as she enjoyed toying with him, this was running longer than she intended. It was time to wrap it up.

"At seventeen, days before you were going to implant that damn chip into my head, I brought you down." Tayes thudded her chest. "Me. A young brown woman brought down The Word!"

"You don't have the wordcast playing in your head?" he asked.

"Of all the cack I've faced, the one thing I never had was you in my head endlessly repeating prayers and affirmations."

"More lies!" He spat on the floor. "Everyone hears The Word."

"I don't."

Randdol squirmed in the chair and leaned back, as if trying to put any distance, even just inches, between them.

"This..." Tayes raised her arms, gesturing past the servers. "Every time you have ever heard a brigader use the term 'citizen,' that was a codename for prisoner. All of Hata is a prison. Every citizen in this city is a convicted war criminal. Haven't you ever wondered why your co-workers or the people you see on the streets are so old? Can you even remember the last time you saw a child or teenager?"

"Of course..." Randdol's cheeks reddened.

"You can't remember any children because there are none. You can't even remember the last time you saw a child." Tayes knew that look. He was reaching his tipping point. The state where he would either shut down and not listen to anything she was saying, or he'd finally believe her. "But let's make this real easy. Tell me how you lost your toe."

"I lost it in The Broken War."

"No," she said. "Your doped up father bit it off."

"That's not right. You are thinking about the story of The Boy and the Rat."

"Who do you think that story is based on?" she asked. "There are some exaggerations, but it's your story. Rat was your dog, and you were the boy born in a horrible war that brought about an even worse one."

Randdol rested his chin on his chest. "I can't remember how I lost my toe." His eyes narrowed, and he looked to the vid screen. Tayes followed his gaze to a parameters box for a single scrubber.

"What?" she asked.

"The scrubbers."

"Yes." Tayes nodded. "That's how we do it. There is no intranet or internet in Hata. The scrubbers directly control the memories people remember and those they don't."

"That's monstrous," he said. "You can't distort and mess with a person's concept of reality. That's sick and twisted."

Tayes agreed. She knew firsthand how horrible it was to control and twist a person's reality, and that's why she believed those who had done such things should be punished for their crimes. "Hata is identical to the way it was the day I took you down. The only difference now is that you are a citizen."

Even the automated wordcast system was exactly as he and his minions had made it. The news reports through the wordcast were all archival and the same ones that Randdol had recorded back in the day. Tayes thought it was fitting that now Randdol was a slave, using the scrubbers on The Words orders to edit his own mind.

"What about Evelyn?" Real concern rang through Randdol's voice. "Have you messed with her head too?"

"Can we lay off Evilyn, as you like to think of her?" Tayes let out a long sigh. "I'm so sick of her cack and your weird obsession over her."

"Evelyn is a goddess!" Randdol rose from his chair. "You take that back. Even if everything else you say is true, I know she would be innocent of all this."

"Evilyn is the worst," Tayes laughed. "And I don't understand why you and her constantly seem to find each other. I swear you have the most cacked up relationship I've ever seen."

"Where is she? What did you do with her?"

"She's in Hata," Tayes said. "We scrubbed her and put her on the other side of the city. Evilyn—"

"Her name is Evelyn! She's an amazing person and beautiful."

Tayes threw a hand up in the air in frustration. "Why does it always have to come back to looks when you talk about your own daughter? See that's—"

"What did you say?"

Tayes hadn't meant to let that bomb drop yet, but the horrific look on Randdol's face made it worth it. His Adam's apple bobbed, and he went sheet white as if he were about to throw up. She hoped he did. "Evilyn is your daughter."

CHAPTER TWENTY-THREE

Randdol tasted bile, but he kept the actual vomit down. This whole ordeal had gone too far. At first, he'd objected to the things that the female brigader was saying. Then he'd played along to get more information out of her. Now... now he felt sick.

He didn't know what to believe anymore. He knew for sure that The Word wasn't real, but had The Word been real? Had he been The Word? No, it wasn't real, just as Evelyn wasn't his daughter. These were just games the woman was playing on him. Probably stalling till more of the brigaders arrived.

The joke was on her though. He'd recorded their entire conversation and streamed it over the wordcast. Whether what she was saying was true or not, the people would hear it and either way they would riot. They would rise against The Brigade. The White Tower would fall.

"You did something, didn't you?" the woman asked. "What was it?"

Randdol figured enough of what they had said had gone out over the cast. He was safe to reveal his trick. "Everything you've said I imported and sent out over the wordcast. The citizens of Hata will know The Word isn't real."

The woman leaned to the side, gazing past him. She checked a second of the vid screens, and then her gun twitched, telling him to turn around. "Go ahead, check out the damage you've caused."

Curious, Randdol spun around to face the vid screen she'd pointed at. "How can I do that?"

"Minimize that vid."

"How?"

She groaned. "Top left corner. Then bring up the cast streams."

He did as she instructed and a grid of live holovids opened. In each of the vids were people, people of all color and ages.

"Try any of them," she said.

Randdol dialed into the first, maximizing the vid. It showed a black man sitting behind a desk. A screen floated beside the man, and on the tiny screen was footage of Randdol sitting in the spinning chair.

"This just in," the black man said. "Hata's most notorious citizen, Randdol Mupt, has been cornered him inside The White Tower. Authorities say he has—"

Randdol flipped to the next cast. A pink-haired girl and a guy in a dress—or at least Randdol thought it was a guy, but he couldn't be sure—were talking. Not wanting to hear what either had to say, Randdol dialed through three more casts, stopping on a video that said, "LIVE FEED."

The screen showed live footage of Randdol sitting in the chair. As Randdol turned to look down at the female brigader, so did the screen Randdol.

"I don't understand," he said. "Why are these people talking about me?"

"The wordcasts are on a locked system," the brigader said. "You can't stream anything to the citizens of Hata that isn't already in the system. What you did was sent live video of our conversation to the outside world."

"This..." he tapped the desk. "These people. These are who live outside the wall? The Opposition?"

The female brigader nodded. "Technically yes, they were at some point The Opposition, but they really are just people."

Randdol rolled through several more channels. The looks of the casters were unreal. Some had skin tones so mashed that he couldn't be sure of their ethnicity. He couldn't remember the last time he had seen someone who wasn't pale or pasty, and now it seemed like more than half of the outside world was just that.

The casters had green hair, blue bangs, sideburns that stretched to the jawbone, tattoos that flickered and played repeating animations, and colorful clothing that looked too bright to be real. Randdol finally stopped on a channel with a middle-aged white guy, though even he was nontraditional with pupils that were slanted like a cat's.

"It was nearly twenty years ago today that The Word was taken down," the man in the cast said. "He and his deplorable cabinet were arrested and have been serving for their crimes as citizens of Hata ever since."

The vid shifted, showing footage of a younger Evelyn. Beside her stood a less wrinkled version of himself. Both wore metal vests that locked their arms behind their backs.

Evelyn's makeup was smudged as if she had been crying. She looked to be somewhere in her twenties. Gone were the crow's feet, and her skin still shined with youth.

"Randdol Mupt and his family were once the most powerful people on the planet," the white man in the vid said. "Let's not forget it was the heroics of a lone teenager who brought them down."

The image shifted again, revealing a young brown girl. Her left arm was in a sling and a bloody bandage covered her right temple, but there could be no mistaking the girl. It was the brigader who now stood behind him.

Randdol minimized the vid casts.

"This is real?" he asked. "You weren't lying? I am The Word? Evelyn is my daughter? Hata is a prison?"

The female brigader nodded.

Vomit shot from Randdol's mouth, but with so little in his stomach, it came out as a dry heave with a cluster of brown bile. His stomached and chest burned.

"Easy there," the female brigader said. "Don't get it on the console."

Randdol didn't know much about the world, but he knew his imprisonment was one of the most cacked up things he'd ever heard of. "What happens now?"

"This isn't the first time you've figured things out. My guess is you'll be scrubbed and sent back to your life, none the wiser."

"How many times has this happened?"

The brigader's head bounced, as if she were counting in her head. "I believe this is the eighth time in seventeen years."

That meant that for seventeen years he, Evelyn, and all the others of the city had been living out fake lives. Caught in an endless loop that offered no hope or escape. It was wrong. He needed to somehow remember. Somehow, he needed to put an end to the cycle. "How did you know I figured it out?"

"Ripping out the transmitters from your teeth was a clue. Removing your tag was also a sign, but honestly, it always comes back to the steak patty."

"The steak patty?" Randdol asked.

"Whenever you are about to do something bad or dangerous, you always eat the steak patty food cartridge."

"It was rotten."

"It wasn't." She shook her head.

"I saw the date," he said. "It was expired."

"It wasn't real." She tapped the side of her temple with the barrel of her gun. "It's all part of the mind games. One of our techs makes it for you. There's always a running pool on when you'll eat it and whether or not you'll vomit."

Randdol once more tasted the steak patty. The memory of the bitter metal with a hint of soured egg made him gag on reflex. His fury surged. Some special cuck who hadn't worked an honest day in their lives had made a joke out of him. They had probably watched the whole thing via hidden cameras in his apartment. His panicking and chugging the rubbing alcohol had most likely been casted to every member of The Opposition. Imprisoning him and playing with his mind was bad enough, but messing with his food had taken things too far.

Randdol leaned back in the chair. This was his life. He was a pawn. A cog inside a system. He did not have free will. He could not live his life or exist the way he wanted. The cycle had to end. He would not go back to Hata. He would die here, and he would take this woman and The Word with him.

CHAPTER TWENTY-FOUR

The one advantage Randdol had was the female brigader did not know he hid a weapon. It sat on the floor, out of her sight, under the desk. The cuck had grown so cocky from reveling in his torture that she'd let her guard down. The gun she'd been pointing at him now was aimed at the floor.

"There is no out for you," the woman said.

Randdol stood. He purposely didn't use the desk or the chair for support, and when he lost his balance, he didn't try to catch himself. He embraced the fall. His stomach smacked the desktop, and he bounced backwards, landing on his butt. Scrambling, he snatched up the gun and aimed it at the stairs.

"Randdol?" the brigader woman stepped on the stairs leading to the console. There was no way she could see him.

He waited, not moving, so she would think he was hurt.

"I'm not stupid, Randdol," the woman said. "Plus, I know you. Come out now with your hands up or I will fire."

Leaning on his side, Randdol cradled the gun against his chest and army-crawled to the stairs. The brigader was gone.

Knowing it was a risk, he rose to his knees.

"Put the gun down." Her voice came from one of the far rows of server towers.

"You aren't in charge here anymore," he yelled back. "I am."

"I will shoot you, Randdol."

The woman had a good point. The one thing she wanted was him. She wanted him incapacitated. She wanted to scrub his mind and put him back into the system. That meant the one thing she didn't want was him dead.

"Your move." Randdol pressed the gun into his chest, aiming the barrel at his heart. "I'd rather die than go back to Hata. So, this is how it will happen. I'm going to count to ten. You will show yourself, and you will set down your gun. If you don't, then when I get to ten, I will fire this into my chest."

"You are bluffing." This time her voice came from the left side of the room. "You're too arrogant to kill yourself."

"I'm not exactly the man you know, just a broken mix of memories and a past I can't remember. So, ask yourself, would the same guy who ripped out two of his own teeth be bluffing right now?" He paused. "One."

Randdol could only hear the noise of the servers and fans.

"Two... three."

He spun, in a slow circle, making sure she wasn't sneaking up behind him.

"Four. Five. Six...."

Randdol moved his finger over the trigger.

"Seven."

Footsteps from the back of the room.

"Eight."

She stepped from the shadows. Her hand was outstretched, with the gun dangling off her pointer and index finger. "Okay, enough. Lower your gun."

"Great idea." He lowered his gun, aimed it at her, and fired.

She rolled to the side, but wasn't fast enough. The spike hit the ground where she'd stood, and the bolts of electricity reached out, striking the nearest tower and her.

The woman convulsed. Her hands flapped around, and she dropped her own gun before going limp. Vomit, purple with little chunks of white things, spewed from her mouth.

Keeping his weapon aimed at her, Randdol approached the woman. He gave her a prod with the tip of his shoes. She didn't respond. He kicked her in the side of the ribs. Again, she didn't move, so he kicked her a third time as hard as he could. There was a cracking sound, possibly her ribs breaking, and still she didn't flinch.

Confident she was out, Randdol bent down and plucked a fire grenade off her belt. He then returned to the other dead brigader and took the two grenades from their belt. Three would do the job nicely, but if he wanted maximum damage, he had to prepare things.

Using the computer, Randdol tracked down which of the server towers held the majority of audio files that made up the wordcast. There were three main towers, on the far back right of the room. To be safe, he intended to throw two of his three grenades in that direction.

He shut down the fire control system, and once ready, dropped the temperature gauge he had meddled with earlier. The last thing he wanted was for a giant fireball to form and then to have the fans blow it out before any damage could be done.

Randdol wished he could see the vids as the casters vented, sighed, or whined about him being dead. They would probably cry because they could no longer torture The Word.

Flipping the first grenade in his hand, he smiled. He was all right with the decision he was making. He didn't see it as killing himself. He saw it as taking back control of his life. This was him winning.

Randdol pressed his thumb into the top of the grenade.

Pain struck his shoulder, and he glanced down to see a bullet stake sticking out of it. His arm went limp, and the grenade fell, rolling down the stairs.

After the second bounce, the female brigader appeared. She dove underneath the grenade, catching it with both hands. The second she did, she twisted and deactivated it.

Randdol wanted to yell at her. He wanted to cuss her out, but lightning from the bullet stake arced up to his face, making everything go numb. His lips swelled, and his vision blurred. The last thing he processed before feeling darkness take him was a warm load of cack releasing from his bowels and filling his pants.

CHAPTER TWENTY-FIVE

Tayes heard crying in the hall. Stepping out of her office, she saw Barbra rushing toward her. Tears streamed down her cheeks.

"What's wrong?" Tayes asked.

"He's a drugged up chronal junkie!" Barbra jumped as if the words she'd spoken had surprised even her. "I'm sorry. I'm a bit flustered. I didn't mean to be vulgar."

"What did Hobbes do?"

"Be careful." Barbra entered her office and locked the door behind her.

Tayes' curiosity was piqued. From down the long hall she could hear things falling over and what sounded like furniture breaking.

Hobbes' usually immaculate office was a wreck. The shelves of old world relics were busted and on the floor. The chairs in front of his desk where tipped. Even the tchotchkes were thrown onto the floor.

Hunched over his desk with his palms flat, he raised his head to meet Tayes' eyes. "You did all of this on purpose, didn't you?"

"Remember that thing you do when you speak nonsense and I have no idea what you're talking about?" Tayes crossed her arms and leaned against the doorframe. "You are doing it again."

"This was it." Spit sprayed from Hobbes' mouth. "You planned all of this."

Tayes had seen many people fall victim to rage. Most were the kind of people who you never suspected it from. Those were the most dangerous ones. It was as if they secretly had a dark hatred repressed deep inside, and when the rage came, it empowered them to do and say the horrible things they'd never had the balls to do before.

Not willing to take a chance, Tayes kept a large distance between herself and Hobbes. She wasn't scared of him. She was worried about having to explain to employee resources why she knocked out her direct supervisor. "Having a bad day, Hobbes? Because I'm sure mine has been worse."

"Don't start that. You love days like today. You love when you get to go rogue. Damn the rules! You are a ratings whore."

"Ahhhh..." She snapped her finger. With everything that had gone down, she hadn't taken the time to scan the holovids. "The streams already covered what happened today?"

"Covering?" He threw his head back and laughed. It was a laugh of the unstable. "You don't get to play that card. You don't get to pretend you're a good person and that this was you doing your job. You used me. You used the system. You are a selfish cuck."

"I take it the board has gotten involved?" She watched him pace behind the desk, his hands shifting back and forth as he opened and clenched.

"Involved?" He drove a fist into his desk. "Weston is on his way now. I already know what's happening. They're promoting you to Warden of Hata."

"I don't want to be warden."

"Keep repeating your pissing lies and maybe you'll eventually believe them."

Hobbes closed the distance, stomping through a yellow puddle on the floor.

Tayes put two and two together, realizing where the musky smell came from. The man had gone batcack and pissed on the floor like he was marking his territory. There could be no doubt. Something had pushed Hobbes full off his rocker and most likely Barbra had been right in claiming he was on eldar juice.

Reaching Tayes, Hobbes stood over her, trying to use his height and girth as intimidation.

"Try me," she said through clenched teeth.

"You're a cacking whore." Hobbes spit on her boots, kicked an antique blue globe, and slammed the office door as he exited.

Tayes shook her head and used the wall for support. Today kept getting worse, and the last thing she wanted was a promotion to Warden. She had never thought about being Warden. She was content as Assistant Warden. Maybe there was a way she could convince the board not to promote her. Maybe she could serve as Acting Warden until a replacement was vetted and found because there was no way Hobbes was keeping the job.

The door opened.

"Oh my word." Weston stood in the doorway. "I've known Gerland for years. I never thought he had this in him."

"Eldar juice," Tayes said.

"That would explain it." Weston extended a hand to Tayes. They shook, and both stepped back to admire the carnage of the room.

"What is that smell?" he asked.

Tayes pointed to the yellow puddle.

Weston winced. "Let's talk somewhere else."

She held an open palm to the door, letting him lead the way.

"How much do you know about the current ratings of Hata's casts?" Weston asked.

"Not much. I focus on the day-to-day aspects of running the city. I don't mess with that kind of stuff."

"Well they've been bad and declining—"

"That makes no sense."

"The war with The Word ended almost twenty years ago." Weston stopped in front of the lift doors and waved his left hand to summon it. "We have grown adults now who weren't alive when it happened."

"Way to make me feel old."

The lift arrived, and they both stepped on.

"History is like that," he said. "I still remember The Broken War. Now, like the war with The Word, it's nothing more than a holovid in a history cast. People are looking forward, not backward, and the interest in a place like Hata has fallen."

The doors to the lift opened onto the roof of The White Tower. Clear curved walls, to diminish the wind gusts, formed a bubble around the roof, while below it was an Eden-like-garden. Cobbled paths led over a bubbling brook and through beds of brightly colored flowers.

"The government offers little funding for Hata," Weston said. "Most of how we make this city work is based on revenue gained from the ratings. In fact, there have been several bills denouncing the city as cruel and unusual punishment—"

"Bullcack," Tayes said. "The people here deserve worse."

"You lived it." Weston sat on an obsidian bench and motioned for her to sit next to him. "Those coming into adulthood don't get it. They don't understand and can't understand what The Word and his people did."

"So, what happens?" Tayes snorted, sucking in a bit of snot that had threatened to slip out her nostril. She wasn't a big fan of the rooftop garden. It always made her sinuses go crazy. "Are we being shut down?"

"No, not yet. Not after a day like today."

"Today was a disaster."

"Today was the best ratings we have had in over ten years. There were hundreds of reaction casts of casters watching our vids!"

"That's good?" she asked.

"It is, and it's why the board voted you Warden."

"I don't want to be Warden."

"We don't care what you want." He rested his hands in his lap. "That sounds harsh, but that's the way of these things."

"Oh?" Tayes stood and moved away from the bench. "So, what do you want?"

"More ratings like today."

"Today should never have happened."

"Maybe it should have?" Weston stroked his chin. "How much do you hate Randdol Mupt?"

"With all my heart."

"Then bring that hate out." He stood and moved to her side, clapping. "Put Randdol through hell every day, and I guarantee the ratings will rise. You will have your everlasting revenge."

"I don't—"

"Don't answer me now. Just know as long as the ratings continue to rise, we don't care how you run the city."

"And if the ratings fall?" she asked.

Weston shrugged. "If they fall much more, I expect the government will step in and The Word and all his cronies will end up in much cushier facilities."

"When do I need to decide?"

"Not now and not to me," he said. "Show me your answer through your actions, not your words."

Weston bowed his head to her. The gesture felt dated, but she understood what he'd meant. To the veterans of The Broken War, it was a sign of respect.

Tayes took her leave, but instead of heading to the lift, she continued to the edge of the garden. Thousands of feet below sprawled Hata. The bay cradled the city, and across the waters were the hint of green treetops, curving around the horizon.

To the east was the great white wall and beyond it was New Hata. Gone were dark drab buildings with hard angles. Instead, she saw the rainbow of reflecting solar panels, luscious parks, and a future she never thought she'd live to see.

As much as she wanted to move on and see the wonders of the world she helped make, she wasn't sure if she was ready. She wasn't sure if she was ready to forgive.

CHAPTER TWENTY-SIX

Randdol woke up before the wordcast told him to. He hated when that happened and credited the waking to a pain he felt in the back of his mouth. The gum around his right and left back molars was inflamed and swollen.

Rolling out of bed, he staggered to the bathroom. His cane was nowhere to be seen. That was a problem. He needed his cane to get through the day.

Opening his mouth, he saw his back molars, and sure enough the marooned gums around the teeth were extra red and agitated. He remembered tripping, maybe? He thought he had tripped. Was that why he didn't see his cane?

He held the side of his head, blinking. Things were foggy as if he were on a high dose of medication.

Making his way to the kitchen, he saw a bill taped to the cabinet. He had to read it twice to make sense of it. It said he owed the city a grand total of 1,425 credit hours. What kind of damn whack service was that? It would take him more than a year to pay off that many hours. Why hadn't someone asked him if he had wanted dental surgery? The city was a mess and no doubt The Brigade was involved. Best to be quiet. It never paid to stir things up with The Brigade.

Randdol's stomach gurgled. He had a sharp pain as if he hadn't eaten in days. Opening the cabinet, he scanned his food cartridges. On the top shelf was a flame grilled steak patty. He reached up to take the cartridge, but then stopped. It was rare, and he should save it for a special occasion. Today wasn't special. Today was just a regular Thursday.

Randdol Mupt hated Thursdays. He also hated all the other days of the week, but it just so happened that today was Thursday, so for today, Thursday was the day he hated the most.

Lindsay Maddings
MCOMM 204
Tayes Heritage University
01.19.84

Essay on the New Resistance:
Learning from the Past to Cope with Now

We live in an enlightened age, or at least that is what some would claim, until this most recent year. Now, our country is in turmoil and the leadership is nothing shy of astounding. In times like this, we must remember our past and have faith in the purity of human nature. We have been through times as horrible as these, and if we remember the lessons of our great grandparents, it will help us once more to regain enlightenment.

It is impossible to talk about resistance in this dark age without first covering the past. Most are familiar with The Brigade. Its rule and downfall are covered in our history books. The holovids and diaries of those times are important historical records, but little coverage is given to how The Brigade gained power.

Randdol Mupt, the fascist autocratic tyrant, rose from nothing during the last great war. Randdol was a conman: from his background as a street rat, to gaining wealth by laundering credits for the chronal mafia, to using that wealth to buy influence, he saw everyone as a rube. At first glance, one might think such a route to power happened only through luck, but his deviousness and use of propagandic gaslighting made it all possible.

The greatest investment Randdol made with his wealth was in developing the casting technology that allowed him to broadcast his gospel to his followers. As the years went by, neuroscience advanced to alter a person's memories, but from the start it was his words that gave him power.

> "Mupt majored in social engineering at university. It was during his course work and research on history that he created his methods of manipulating a person's perspective on reality" (Colony 10.44.08).

The methods Mupt used were straightforward. He began by denouncing the press, the government, and social media sites that covered news in a way he did not like. It was in these early years he coined the phrase "Trust the Word," which literally meant that his followers should believe him over all other media outlets. With his enormous wealth, gained from illegal laundering, he had the best lawyers, and if anyone disagreed or claimed his words were lies, he would sue them. He painted himself as an underdog fighting a broken system, and the lawsuits, even though they never went to trial, made it appear he was in the right. He would bury his opponents in paperwork until the next crisis or drama revealed itself. It was his image that mattered, not the cases (Burke 20.113).

The turning of the masses and convincing the public that no one else but Mupt himself spoke the truth synchronized his rise to power. With millions following him, and the creation of the wordcasts, nothing could stop him. The casts systematically spread his falsehoods. Even those who were sane were so inundated with the lies they questioned their own reality.

> "Mupt's gaslighting propaganda was simple. Every day he and his supporters would insist the sky was red. It didn't matter that you could see the sky and knew it was blue. Thousands of times you'd hear it was red and the onslaught of those lights would eventually make you question your own

sanity. Maybe the sky was red, and you weren't seeing it right?" (Hata Now 1784.1)

There were other factors that led to Mupt gaining and holding power, especially events on the world stage, but at the core it was his ability to con the masses into believing his lies and spreading them to others that brought him power. That means if we wish to prevent a new Word from rising, we need to start by ensuring the truth is always shared.

When a person does not want to believe what you tell them, it is hard to get them to accept the truth. Accepting the truth requires critical thinking and having the intelligence and emotional awareness to evaluate one's own thoughts. Outlined below are four main steps a person can use to help not only fight lies, but repair our broken system. These are the same steps used to fight The Word and what led to his downfall.

The most important thing a person can do when resisting is to educate themselves and others. Crises like the one that lead to The Word make individuals insecure and question reality. The best way to fight is for a person to boost their self-esteem and nothing does that better than knowledge.

THU published a new study where they placed a thousand students into three groups. The first group was given true news stories. The second group was only given false news stories. The third group was given both true and false stories. Seventy-two percent of the first group believed the true news stories. Sixty-nine percent of students from the second group believed the false news stories. However, eighty-six percent of students given both the false stories and true stories ended up believing the true stories (THU Today 10.3.38).

What this study proves is the importance of critical thinking in fighting falseness. A person, when giving two opposing pieces of information, is more likely to believe the truth than someone who is only given true stories. Thus, to educate yourself and to help awaken others, keep in mind that the best way to do so is to become an omnivore by exposing yourself to multiple viewpoints.

The second most important thing a person can do when resisting is to support the free press. To have multiple viewpoints and to stop gaslighting there must be those out there who will speak and publish the truth. Whether a person is a fan of holovids, casts, or digital periodicals, it is important that those outlets are funded. The first thing Mupt did when rising to power was disband the press.

Free press is essential to a democratic system. Free press creates accountability. Accountability, being held responsible for the things you do and say, keeps those in power from lying and hiding important information from the public. Without a free press, any information a government publishes has the potential to be nothing more than propaganda.

> "We saw it when Randdol Mupt took power. Without the press, there was no one to speak out against his lies. There was no one to question the disinformation and without that he ran wild" (Carter 10B).

The final lesson we can take from the rise of Mupt is that if a person disagrees with what is happening, then they should speak out. New anti-protesting laws and social pressure continue to move us closer to reliving The Word. Those in power want citizens to fall victim to that social stigma. They want to silence voices.

> "There are three core ways a citizen may speak out. First, they can take part in non-violent lawful protests. Second, they can contact their local lawmakers through meetings and traditional communications. Third, they can write letters, as well as create holovids and casts expressing views so that the ruling powers are never normalized" (Picer 103.481).

However, no matter how a citizen expresses their voice, it is important to keep in mind that without an overall message, protests or casts can be the equivalent of shouting at a wall. Context matters. Protesting at a clothing boutique about genetic augmentation of domesticated animals might not be as powerful as doing it at a trade show for restaurant owners. On the other hand, contacting your local lawmaker and complaining about shoe prices will do a person little good. To maximize a voice being heard, consideration of having a clear message and choosing the best way to deliver the message is important.

Freedom of the press creates accountability for a government, but attending town hall and messaging your local lawmaker creates accountability on a micro scale. A lawmaker is more likely to vote in your interest when they know not doing so will cost them your vote and the votes of those that agree with you.

> "The key is to not give into despair. The other side, the so-called opposition, wants that. They want you to feel hopeless. They want you to feel like your voice doesn't matter. They want you to give up. By giving up you give them the power" (Siaggot 21.084A).

After the fall of The Word, no one thought a threat like this would happen again. Now here we are. It is a reminder to those who claim enlightenment and those with the ability to think critically: Fight for what you believe in. Learn from our great grandparents' mistakes and take to heart how they stood up for all.

With the recent election, our country has started a new dark era, but it has been down this road before, and by taking the lessons of the past, the citizens can ensure its recovery and stability. By being educated, supporting the free press, and making voices heard, you can help resist.

Want to know how a 17-year-old Catherine Tayes took down The Word? Join the author's mailing list and get RESISTED, an exclusive bonus story!

GET IT NOW!

http://www.scottking.info/blog/resisted/

AUTHOR NOTE

I'm a super sniffer. The technical diagnosis is that I have hyperosmia, a heightened sense of smell. It means if I'm around any kind of smoke, I'll get a sinus infection, or if I walk through the perfume section of a department store, I might break into a sneezing fit. For the most part, on a day-to-day scale, almost everything smells bad or too strong. It sucks.

The benefit of being a super sniffer is that I have an amazing sense of taste. When Lisa, my wife, and I sit down to eat, she might be able to tell you that the red sauce on the pasta tastes good, but I'll be able to pick out the layers of garlic, oregano, the hint of cayenne pepper, or whatever else went into it.

My father was a chef, and I grew up in two restaurants, so at this stage in the game I know food and my hyperosmia gives me a special insight. It's also probably why food plays a big part in a lot of the stories I write. Last year when I penned the first book in an epic fantasy series, I actually took the time to create recipes so that I knew the different foods and style of cooking that regions of that world used. It's also probably why food plays such a large part in RESIST THEM.

For the most part, I'm not picky when it comes to food. I draw the line at two things. I hate green peas with a passion because of their smell. They have a musky sour scent like rancid yeast mixed with toe jam. I also don't like frozen or boxed meals because to me they taste as if they are ninety percent preservatives, which is just gross.

When writing RESIST THEM, I knew I wanted to beat down Randdol with food. I wanted to crush him. That's one of the reasons why his go-to meal is mashed peas stew. The idea of a mashed pea stew sounds so utterly gross to me. I also thought it would make a fantastic contrast to the raspberries when he finally got to eat one.

I partially wanted to really oversell the taste of the raspberries when he ate them, but when I got to that scene, I hit a bit of a snag. Raspberries have such a distinct flavor that it is hard to describe what they taste like without simply saying they tasted like raspberries, and you can't use a word to describe a word. That's just bad writing. So I ended up having to trim down the description of the flavor a bit more then I had originally intended.

The steak cartridge that Randdol tastes was really just me being mean, because that's what you have to do as an author, but I did have fun trying to figure out what it should taste like. I've learned that people in general don't respond well when you describe what food taste like with non-food things. So if you want something to taste bad, you need to describe it with things that people can't or shouldn't eat.

For example, I could say something like, "I drank a milk shake and it tasted like a gritty fishing line." Then even if you don't know what a gritty fishing line tastes like, you are probably imagining something bad and wincing. That's the power of taste!

Sometimes I feel guilty for making my characters eat horrible things, but those times are generally balanced with them getting to eat good stuff. It's just that RESIST THEM is a bit of a dystopian, so there was a bit more bad than good. My next book is not nearly as dark, and I promise to have lots of yummy tasting things in it!

ABOUT THE AUTHOR

Scott King is a writer, photographer, and educator. He was born in Washington, D.C. and raised in Ocean City, Maryland. He received his undergraduate degree in film from Towson University, and his M.F.A. in film from American University.

Until moving to Texas to follow his wife's career, King worked as a college professor, teaching photography, digital arts, and writing-related classes. He now works full time as a game photographer and author.

As a board game photographer, King shoots games for websites, online stores, and for other marketing needs. He also produces an annual calendar that highlights board and other hobby games.

To learn more about Scott and his work, visit his website at www.ScottKing.info. You can also follow him on Twitter via @ScottKing.

BOOKS BY SCOTT KING:

Holiday Wars
Holiday Wars Volume 1: The Holiday Spirit
Holiday Wars Volume 2: Winter's Wrath
Holiday Wars Volume 3: Queen's Gambit
Holiday Wars Volume 4: Shadow Taken

Zimmah Chronicles
Cupcakes vs. Brownies
Mermaids vs. Unicorns
Genie vs. Djinn

Finish the Script!
The 5 Day Novel
DAD! A Documentary Graphic Novel
National Cthulhu Eats Spaghetti Day
The Eye of Hastur
Ameriguns

NOTE TO THE READER

Thank you for reading *Resist Them*. If you enjoyed the book, I hope you'll consider leaving a review. They're the lifeblood of indie authors and the most important factor for other readers in deciding if they will pick it up.

This book is a work of fiction. Any reference to historical events, real people, or real locales are used facetiously. Other names, characters, places, and incidents are the product of the author's imagination, and any resemblance to actual events or locales or persons, living or dead, is entirely coincidental.

RESIST THEM

Published by Majestic Arts

Cover Photos & Design by Scott King

Edited by Clark Chamberlain

Manufactured in the United States of America

Copyright ©2017 Scott King

ISBN: 1546405895

ISBN-13: 978-1546405894

First Edition: May 2017

All rights reserved. No part of this book may be reproduced in any form or by any means without permission in writing from the author, except for the inclusion of brief quotations in a review.

Printed in Great Britain
by Amazon